Hippocrene U.S.A. Guide

RV

Hippocrene U.S.A. Guide

RV
Travel Leisurely
Year Round

Rollanda D. Masse

HIPPOCRENE BOOKS
New York

Acknowledgments

I want to sincerely thank my father, Lucien Dumais; my sister, Denise Aboud; my friends, Andrée Neveu, Louise Landry, Bernice Moreault and Myrelle DiRosa, who have helped me to translate my French book *La Vie Nomade* into this book. And also Furio for his patient help.

My very special thanks to dear Mrs. Jane Ferrier, a friendly retired English teacher who patiently edited my French-style English prose.

The names of organizations, firms and products are given to assist the reader and not as an endorsement. Some of the items described may change before the book is in print.

Of necessity, the publisher and author assume no liability or responsibility concerning information about services rendered by any of the organizations, firms and products listed.

For information, contact:
HIPPOCRENE BOOKS, INC.
171 Madison Avenue
New York, NY 10016

ISBN-0-87052-958-7

Printed in the United States of America.

In loving memory for my husband,
Lucien Masse,
with whom I started this nomad life.

Contents

Introduction

How would you like to view the world while enjoying all the comforts of home? Travel and live year long as you please, without packing a suitcase or taking care of a house?

The rich and the famous own homes all over. They have to find trusty managers to look after their houses and hire secretaries to see that what is needed for their comfort is hauled wherever they go. Even so, a celebrity may not have with her the royal blue sequin dress she would suddenly like to wear on a certain evening.

I do not need an entourage of employees, and I, nevertheless, own a house in Texas, one in Mexico, one in Florida, one in Canada; and in spite of my modest income, I can have one almost anywhere I wish.

You've guessed it! I'm talking about a house on wheels, the mini-motorhome in which I live all year. I drive it at the pace I want and park it where I want to stay a day, a week or whatever pleases me. I have "instant residency" anywhere! It is simple as can be!

During the past few years, I have had experience with about every peculiar situation of this lifestyle. I have also learned much from the hundreds of other nomads I have met and through the literature I get from all my contacts in this wonderful world of life on wheels.

This book is my attempt to answer the questions I'm always asked and show you how you too can be free and live this happy way.

CHAPTER 1

Who Is Living and Traveling in These Houses on Wheels?

Modern Nomads

Modern nomads are what we are, I and thousands of other happy wanderers. We live in houses on wheels all year. We have no other residences; these are our homes! We consider them sufficient because we have found out they contain everything we really need. It is primarily the free, easy lifestyle that I am writing about in this book.

We wanderers are often called "snowbirds," like the little birds who each winter migrate to a warm climate. We have found an independent and economical lifestyle in the comfort of the southern sun, while our friends up north suffer through the long winter, cooped up in their houses or fighting the snow and the cold.

Most nomads do not try to convert anybody else (I am one

of the exceptions), but most of us are ready to talk about our kind of life to the people who are interested.

If you have used a recreational vehicle for an occasional trip, you might think that living in one would not be practical. That's understandable because when you go on holiday you do not have all your belongings with you; you take only what you think you will need for the trip. You do not have the cooking utensils you need, the shoes that would look so great, the book you have time to read—and you do not remember in which corner you shoved the binoculars! Furthermore, you are driving a lot, almost constantly, because your vacation time is limited, and you have to get to your destination as soon as possible. And if it rains. . . . it's a catastrophe because you have no time to lose! You should be on the beach, not confined indoors with nothing to do!

Imagine now that you are a fulltime nomad. First, you would probably be in another vehicle better suited to your needs, with all the effects necessary for a regular day to day life. Second, you would have lots and lots of time to go where you want to go, see what you want to see and visit whomever you want to be with.

If you were a fulltime nomad, on rainy days, you might go to a local library and look up information on your recently acquired hobby. You could do your shopping or go to a movie, stay at home and answer a few letters, or re-organize a drawer and hem a pair of pants while watching the TV. When a house on wheels (recreational vehicle or RV) is your home, you live almost like you do in an ordinary house, except that you have so much less cleaning and maintenance to do that you have plenty of time to enjoy the outdoors, visit friends and family and pursue your hobbies. In fact, you have time to do what you *like*; you are free. . . . Think about it.

Retirees

In recent years we have heard much about leisure. We are encouraged to have hobbies and to exercise for our mental, as well as our physical, well-being. Still, some people live only to work; they do nothing else. However, with time, the majority have learned to take advantage of shorter working weeks and longer vacations, and fill their leisure time with activities they enjoy. Many middle-aged people think of early retirement. They have developed a variety of pleasurable interests and wish they had more free time to enjoy themselves.

People now live longer; they are in better shape and look younger at seventy-five than people of sixty did fifty years ago. So, it's no surprise that many retirees have included RVing in their retirement plans. Eventually, thousands, perhaps millions of them (no one knows for sure) decide to simplify their lives by using their RVs all year round. It becomes truly a *R*esidence *V*ehicle.

Let me tell you about some friends of mine who have made this decision. They are members of camping clubs to which I belong:

Pat and Connie like this type of life so much that when they are asked where and when they will settle down, they answer, "Somewhere in the U.S.A., and not before we are forced to." Connie says she is not ready to go back to a house. "Now, by the open window just over our bed, we breathe the scent of the flowers or the fresh air of the sea, and we hear the birds singing. We live right in the midst of nature.

"If in the morning we decide we want another setting. . . . no problem! Even if we go only twenty miles farther, when we take to the road again (Pat leans over and touched my hand and we look at each other). Both of us share this marvelous feeling of freedom: we are free of the telephone, of schedules and commitments. What a nice life!"

Barry and Kate say, "We have lived and traveled fulltime in a thirty-two foot trailer since October 1986, we have spent the winters visiting the Southwestern states. We have met people of all professions, from all walks of life, who live in their RVs. They all have this in common: they enjoy life fully and the oldest ones are young olders. This life is for us."

Bud and Marilyn told me, "We have been fulltime nomads for ten years. We have visited all the states and all the provinces. We made more friends while traveling than during all the years we were busy working." (They attended the first rally my late husband and I organized for the Escapees Club. They are warm and friendly; no wonder they make so many friends!)

Duane and Bev recall, "We met John and Dot at a campground last June. They told us about their lifestyle. One month later, we put our house up for sale and it sold in two weeks! We have just purchased this brand new trailer and truck, and are very excited about this new life we have just started."

Norm and Betty feel, "We have just resumed our nomad life of four years. About two months ago, we decided to stay put and raise chickens, or something like that. We were about to sign the deed on a thirteen-acre farm when we suddenly realized we would go nuts living all the time in the same place. So we're on the road again."

Al and Mary reminisce, "We've sold the piano, sold the kitchen table and the chairs, sold the bed and the dressers. We had to sleep in our trailer even before the house was sold. Then we went to Spokane in mid-May, to Glacier Lake Macdonald in mid-June, to Chicago in mid-something. This is the life!"

And there are the super nomads. People who have met *Vic and Vi White* (I met them) will never forget this couple. Here is what has been said about them:

Traveling around the world to sixty different countries in their motorhome, sharing their experiences in books and also highly interesting slide presentations, they have accomplished what most of us dream of doing but think impossible. The word *impossible* does not exist in their vocabulary. Proof is the time Vic moved the steering of his big motorhome to the right side. Several people watching him work, told him it was impossible. Two months later, he was driving from the right side of his RV! They drive this way, on the left side of the road, in his native Australia, the land to which they were returning after twenty-five years of being nomads. Now that they are eighty-five, some think they plan to settle down. . . . Oh no! They will keep traveling, rediscovering their own country. They are proof that nothing is impossible.

Lone Travelers

Above us, a black sky studded with stars that seemed particularly close to us on that beautiful July evening. In front of us, the dancing flames of a campfire around which a dozen of us nighthawks were nattering. The conversation switched from places to see to traveling tips to the very funny anecdotes of a certain Joe from Maine. Everybody was laughing heartily.

As silence returned, a young lone nomad from Texas (Ray, about seventy-five years old) leaned back on his chair while pushing back his cowboy hat and exclaimed, "I can't believe it! Here I am, in Montreal, at half past midnight, having a good time with fellow campers from all over! If I had stayed in the town where I retired, I would probably have been asleep since 9:30 in that retirement home I go to once a year to see my former colleagues. What a good life I have chosen . . . We all have chosen!"

This was in 1985, in Hudson near Montreal, where Lucien, my husband, and I had invited the Escapees Club. Since then I was recently widowed and a member of the Loners on Wheels Club, twenty-four singles of this club had joined the rally on my invitation. My heart was not really in the organization of this event, but my friends from FQCC, a local camping club helped me enormously and we all had a good time.

Yes, there are many who travel alone in RVs! The majority are occasionals because they have a home, an apartment, a house, a cottage or a mobile home. But, there are hundreds who, like me, are fulltime nomads. There are even many who, like me, do not own a car. Their motorhome, mini-motorhome, van or camper is their car!

Please meet a few singles:

Lou lives in a thirty-three foot motorhome. He travels mainly in the eastern U.S.A. He is a retired Eastern Airlines pilot. He started flying in 1939 and served in the Air Force as a flying instructor and squadron assistant commander. In 1946, he became a captain for Eastern. He was the pilot of a hijacked plane and consequently was involved in security programs for airlines and airports. He has used his talents many times as a writer and speaker to promote more secure air travel. Lee has six children and eight grandchildren.

Rita has been fulltiming nine years in her motorhome. A retired personnel consultant, she spends winters in Tucson and summers on the road. She enjoys travel, reading, fishing, birding, sewing and handicrafts. She also takes photographs for lectures and slide shows. Rita has two children and one grandson.

Ray lives in his thirty-three foot motorhome. He spent twenty-seven years in the U.S. Army and enjoys improving his RV, swimming, playing tennis and talking on his ham radio.

Hazel says, "I am now a fulltime nomad. I've sold my house to my neighbor. He said I could come and park in his driveway anytime. I feel free; I never felt so good!"

Les travels in his motorhome. Retired as a corporate executive, he spends winters in the South and summers in the North and Northwest of both the U.S. and Canada.

Dorothy, who is seventy, has traveled in a twenty-six foot motorhome since 1971. She has been state director of the

Good Sam Club, and plays the electronic organ and the accordian at many club rallies.

Mickey? She is traveling fulltime, pulling a fifth-wheel trailer. Nothing to it for a widow like Mickey! After all, she is only eighty-two!

We do not like to think about it, but one of these days, death will break up the couple that we are. A man who finds himself alone is really taken by surprise; the statistics always told him that his wife would most certainly be by his side until his last day. Many women probably never consider what they will do if their husbands die. One day, they find themselves alone, in a hall filled with couples. Wherever they go, there seem to be only couples. Well, if you've loved RVing with a partner, there is no reason to quit because you are alone.

Consider this: In conventional social life, couples rarely will invite a widow to join them at a restaurant, to go dancing, to play cards. They are naturally inclined to invite couples. There are only a few close couples a widow can phone and see once in a while . . . and only at first. Soon with most couples, a woman gets the impression she is imposing in a situation that is not comfortable anymore.

In campgrounds, however, everyone talks to anyone at the pool or at the recreation hall, and as a camper, you know you belong. With camping club rallies, it is easy; you do not have to wait to be invited, you are invited when you read the club newsletter. And if you are a member of a club for singles, it is even better; every other member is in the same situation!

There are quite a few camping clubs for singles. One is called Loners on Wheels or LOWs. (You cannot attend their functions with a partner of the opposite sex in your unit). This is probably the largest singles club; they have rallies going on all the time all over the United States and sometimes in Canada. Hundreds of members spend the winter in a section of the Slabs, in California, where they stay for a one-time fee of $25, like the thousands of other campers there. LOWs own two parks: one in California and the other in Florida. Members can camp for a small fee or purchase a lot for about $6,000. Members receive logo stickers, a newsletter, and membership directory, along with a list of rest areas that provide dumping stations.

Note: *You do not have to be a fulltime nomad to become a member of any clubs mentioned in the book.*

Here is a sampling of the comments of some single ladies:

Bernice: "We were a caravan of five traveling for a week in Northeastern Arizona. We saw the Petrified Forest, the Painted Desert and the Indian Reserve at De Chelly Canyon, where we visited the ruins—this was something! And we met Cathy, an expert fisherman(??) at Wheatfield Lake, where she cooked fresh trout for us. Delicious! I hope to travel again with LOWs."

Mary: "This past year has been full of discoveries for me in California, Arizona, Utah and Colorado. I have met many LOWs and attended a few rallies. I am on my way to Rio Grande, Texas, where I intend to sell my mobile home. I do not need it; I prefer RVing year-round."

Lea: "I will escape the working world when I pre-retire in October. But I have so many projects and with my joining committees of the SKP (Escapees) and LOWs clubs, I guess I will be busier than now, but it's going to be fun, fun, fun. . . ."

For the singles who prefer the option of having a companion of the opposite sex in their RVs, there are other groups. To members of the Family Motor Coach Association (FMCA) the Single International Chapter offers a newsletter and organized rallies. Here is what Pete Moore, the president, says:

> Sure, most of us are hoping to find the ideal partner but it is primarily the fact that we are all in the same situation that links the members. I have been alone for quite a while, and often feel like the fifth wheel among couples. And for once in a group of singles, there are more men than women! Often,

members double up in an RV for company as well as to share the expenses.

A new club that is expanding rapidly and reflects its founder's enthusiasm is WIN (What *I* *N*eed to know). It is for singles *born after 1926.* If you join, Dorothy Prince will send you a badge, a sticker and a regular newsletter which will tell about the rallies and will include what she calls the Wandering *I*ndividuals' *N*etwork, letters from members.

Last summer, as I stepped down from my mini-motorhome in a shopping center lot, a lady came up to me and said in a tone of disbelief, "You're driving this yourself?"

"I have to," I said. "My husband passed away, so I am alone now."

"Don't tell me you travel in this alone?"

"Yes," I said, "year-round, this is my home and my car."

Well, she thought I was joking; then she started to ask me all kinds of questions. She confessed, "Since my husband died, almost one year ago, I have not touched the motorhome. In fact, yesterday I put an ad in the paper to sell it. What a strange thing that I should meet you today. Now that I have talked with you, I'm convinced that I too can drive my motorhome by myself. I think I'll keep it."

I gave her application forms for the clubs I belong to. When she left, all excited, she said she would write to them immediately.

"So, we might meet again," I said, thinking probably not. Well, as I was rewriting this book in English, my mail came one day. And guess what? I had a letter from this lady. She described our meeting and told me that she had read my book, the one published in French, *La Vie Nomade.* What a coincidence! She said she was traveling in her RV by herself and planned to sell her home next summer. And, I will see her again. She will be at a club rally that I also plan to attend in Florida.

So, try it alone. You will have a more exciting life! And if you prefer to have a partner (it's not easy to find the right one, I know) there is the personal column in the Good Sam Club's newspaper, as well as other sources.

Pre-Retirees

Many people in their sixties say (and everyone I've asked agrees) that if they had known it was so easy and so inexpensive, they would have retired much earlier, and at a younger age; they probably would have enjoyed retirement then even more.

Some have done it! A few weeks ago, in Lexington, Texas, I met Ken and Betty. They are in their early forties; they met at a Mensa meeting and they have been married eleven years now. Two years ago, they sold everything and bought a beautiful thirty-foot motorhome. They use it to pull a large trailer containing two expensive motorcycles and all their paraphernalia. "Now we have time to really talk to each other and do what we want," Ken said.

His computer is right in front of a comfortable chair. Ask him the date of the next rally of a club, or how much he spent on gas last month, and he can give you the answer after pressing a few keys.

After Betty played a sonata on her folding piano, I asked Ken if he played an instrument. To my surprise he played some Chopin on his computer!

He is an expert in motorhome maintenance of necessity. He says that learning by reading about all the tricks to save money on the road is what has made it possible for them to afford pre-retirement, and to enjoy it. They plan to attend a Mensa convention in Montreal and want me to be their guest. It should be great!

Here is what *Pat and Lauretta* say: "This retirement on wheels at fifty years old is marvelous! We are new campers, and this life pleases us tremendously! We have sold our house and live now, happy and comfortable, in our twenty-three-foot mini-motorhome. We now are on the road to New Mexico."

Bill told me, "Three years ago, at fifty-two, I was a detective with a police department when I learned that my retirement check at that time would be 60% of my salary. So, I thought, if I keep my job, I'll be working for only 40%. It's not worth it. I added up all the money I would save by not eating out all the time because of the job, by my wife not needing a car because she would have the use of mine, and by saving about half on my income tax. It totalled much more than 60%. So I quit and became an early retiree. We have not felt money restricted at all, and, besides, we had all this free time! Unfortunately, my wife died not long after, so we could not enjoy it together very long.

In Montreal, Canada, during the summer of '87, Bill came from Arkansas to attend a singles rally I had organized. He commented, "Now that I am a nomad, living only in my thirty-three-foot motorhome, I am almost rich!"

In 1982, my husband and I met Don and Sue Dulaney in a New Jersey campground where they were camped next to us. When we told them we were living year long in our thirty-foot motorhome, they said they did not know people lived that way. But, they decided right then to eventually try it. We kept in touch; they would write: "Two more years to wait. . . ." and so on, until, at age fifty-five, Don retired, sold the house, bought a new motorhome and took to the road with the happy Sue. They were just here, last week, telling me all about their happy wanderings. They also gave me some good suggestions for this book. Thank you, my good friends!

Working Nomads

Chuck and Ginny told me, "When we were married three years ago, Chuck had a dream; he wanted to teach at a school in a different state every year. It sounded like fun. We attended recreational vehicle shows to decide which RV would suit this lifestyle. But every time we mentioned our project, people looked at us as if we were crazy. We were beginning to think that maybe we were until one day we met a fulltime nomad who explained his own lifestyle and reassured us. If we are a bit crazy, now we know there are thousands who must also be."

Carl and Betty became fulltime nomads when she was thirty-two and he, thirty-four. He was working for a plumbing contracting firm and she was teaching; during the summers, she worked in an office. Carl said:

It took us two years to get ready. We were spending our annual two-week vacations in our trailer, but every year it was becoming more difficult to return to work. We liked to go camping on weekends but hated to have to rush home each Friday, pack the trailer, and drive most of the evening to get to secluded places. We came back late on Sunday nights; and after unpacking and putting everything away, we fell into bed completely exhausted. I had to get up the next morning at five and work all week to be able to rush to go camping on the next weekend. And there were those weekends when I had to stay home to fix the house or garden. . . . And the winter . . . We didn't like winter sports, but hated to stay inside, hated to shovel snow, or fight with the car that would not start. . . .

I had a lot of stress at work, and a couple of guys wanted my job as supervisor. Arriving home one evening, I said to Betty that I would not care if I ever returned to work. She asked me why I did not resign.

I took a pencil and began to make some calculations. By selling the house, the furniture and one car, adding the money to our savings, once the total was invested, we would have a monthly income of $600. If we were careful, we were sure we could manage on that.

We sold everything and hit the road in our trailer. Often we have stayed in very nice campgrounds after negotiating an exchange with the owner or the manager. I cut wood with my electric saw, or Betty substitutes for the owner's wife in the office, and we stay for free. We have picked tomatoes, oranges and apples for minimum wages; but, what the heck! We parked free on the farm, in a warm and healthy climate and we could always quit any time we wanted.

We stop in little towns and talk to storekeepers, gas station owners, etc., and tell them what we can do. Soon, someone offers us a job. In the campgrounds, many retired people are very happy to find someone who will do the jobs they cannot or don't want to do. We have made many good friends since we've started living like this. After an enjoyable visit, we do not like to part with them, but we know we will probably see them again in Florida, Texas or Arizona. There is an older couple that we call Pa and Ma. We have met them four times here and there, and we always feel a little bit like they are our parents.

We "boondock" a lot, camping where there is no water, electricity or sewers, because those places are free, and we can pick a very private spot if we want. We take time to go fishing and to visit Indian museums, our latest interest. We are free to work or to loaf, to stop or to go. We love this life a hundred times more than living in our suburban bungalow, always wishing we were free.

My very favorite "working-traveling with kids" full-timers are undoubtedly *Joe and Kay Peterson.* I have met them many times, and have great affection and a lot of admiration for this exceptional couple. It was a few months after we had been living fulltime in our motorhome that my husband Lucien and I saw an ad for the Escapee Club and learned that other people were also living in their RVs. Joining the club and reading its newsletters and Kay's books (*Home Is Where You Park It, Survival Of the Snowbirds* and Joe's and Kay's *Encyclopedia for RVers*) improved our RV life tremendously. It pleases me to know that they have been successful at what they are doing.

For Christmas 1969 they had received a gift subscription to

Trailer Life and their dream of fulltime RVing was born. Unable to afford a new trailer of the type they wanted, they settled for a used 1959 Airstream that was in good shape. Joe's plan was to use it occasionally for the next few years, but with only three children remaining in the nest, Kay convinced him that they didn't have to wait until all the children finished school. In June 1970, they began fulltiming. With Joe's membership in a union trade, finding work was no problem. During the seventies, electrical construction was at its peak throughout the country. Joe could quit a job on a Friday, travel during the weekend, and start a new job on Monday.

They remained in one place for a school semester, doing most of their traveling during the summer. The story of those years is told in *Home Is Where You Park It*.

Kay says, "Taking off, as we did, is a risk. It is not for those whose goal is to make a lot of money. We gave up the security of paid health insurance (she is a nurse) and a union pension that is part of the reward given to "wage slaves." But we had no desire for a Rolls Royce—a Chevy pick-up took us anywhere we wanted to go.

"We started the Escapee Club," Joe adds, "as a way to keep in touch with those we met in our travels. The club's continued growth has changed our lifestyle. After all these years as full-timers, we are back to being part-timers. Even with our present staff of fourteen people, Kay and I still devote most of our time to the club."

"But we have no regrets," Kay adds. "Our life has been—and continues to be—a grand adventure."

Suggestions of the Working Nomads

If you want to stay put for a few days or a few weeks because you plan to explore the area, or because your paintings are being shown in a town, or for any other hobby you pursue, you can park free. There may be someone who will be grateful to have an RV parked on his property to deter vandalism while he is away on a trip. So, in addition to free parking, you may get water, electricity and sewer, or the use of a phone and pool, in exchange for watering the lawn and feeding the dog. You can also offer your presence to building contractors, stores, schools, etc.

One thing is important if you try this: you should have a contract.

As you will learn in a coming chapter, you can camp free at many places. But if you want to spend some time in a campground, and enjoy the pool and all the facilities for free, you can offer your services to the manager. Always try to park near the office, the recreation hall, or the main campground road.

With the permission of the manager you can use the bulletin board to advertize your talents. Most renderers of service in the parks I have been in were not setting prices. Generally, they were asking for a donation, or would say, "Usually people give me $. . . ." It should be lower than the local competition, of course.

One ad I have often looked for and never found when I needed it is: Sewing and alterations, see Lucy, lot 42. (I know, it's hard to believe; you would think many ladies would be interested.) Other suggestions of services you might provide are:

Let me and my typewriter update your correspondance.
Go out! Have fun! I'll babysit.
Let me finish your knitting or other handicraft.
We do windows and complete housecleaning.
Haircuts for men and women.
Small house repairs, exterior maintenance.
We'll cook your meals, do your errands.

Another possibility might be making bread and cakes. The aroma alone would bring you business faster than a temporary sign on your RV! What about giving lessons? Maybe you know something the majority of us would like to learn! The owner or manager will probably be delighted to offer more activities in the camp. It will cost him nothing, the students will take care of the expenses! So what if you do not do something as well as the professionals on TV? Everyone will have fun trying a new activity, including you, who perhaps will be a teacher for the first time. And if it does not catch on, remember the saying:

> Failures are the battle scars
> of those who tried
>
> —Unknown

A few ideas for lessons include: sewing, knitting, bridge, art, photography, golf, fishing, candlemaking, flower drying, exercise, swimming, ballroom or line dancing, and macrame.

Even if you instruct for only a few sessions, you may want to have more information. A bookstore or the local library will be able to help you find more information on the subject you want to teach. Who knows? You might become a real pro, if you're not one already. The important thing is to enjoy what you are doing. The primary reason to be a nomad is to leave the stress back home, remember?

For instance, suppose you love to make dolls, but don't make much money selling them, or you like fishing on a pier, talking to everybody, and selling them your hooks and lures. If these few dollars are enough and you spend nice days doing what you like, it is an ideal set-up. You cannot ask for a better job! If you need more money and have to do something you do not really enjoy, at least, try to find work that pays well in a short period of time. And change activities often, so you do not get bored.

Some suggestions from experienced nomads:

- In a campground, advertise RV carpet cleaning ($9 to $15 according to the size). Take at least five customers the same day. Rent a machine with accessories for corners (about $15). Collecting an average of $12 from five people, you earn $45 for a day's work. Considering the low cost of living as a nomad, you do not have to work many days in a week.

- Choose a quiet business day and offer to wash store windows. You will average about $15 an hour, and the necessary equipment is minimal.
- Visit car dealers and offer to sell them plastic pennants which you will install. (Be sure there is no current in any wires you touch.)
- Offer to paint the prices on windshields of cars for sale. It's easy to get the knack of it!
- Paint signs for special sales on store windows; you will be especially welcome just before Christmas.
- Take photographs of people attending a special dinner, dance, rally, golf tournament or even a cruise. Develop them on location with a kit you purchase at a camera shop. Mount them as key chains or badges and sell them for $5 each or 2 for $9. Many people would buy them as mementos of a happy time and it would be a profitable evening for you.
- On a sunny, quiet Sunday morning, take pictures of the facades of small stores. Most owners do not have a picture of their stores. You could offer them mounted in 8" × 10" or 3" × 5" sizes for $15 or more. If a merchant is not interested, come back another day. Offer to trade the photos for merchandise or service, say a haircut. It works!

There are all kinds of mobile businesses you can get involved in. You can sell small RV parts or name badges or plates. One good source of ideas is the newsletters and magazines from the different camping clubs. I once saw an ad for a donut machine. It suggested that a person could easily make and sell fresh donuts.

Good advice for working nomads is never to forget to barter (negotiate an exchange) when it can benefit you. Also, do not complicate your life by working or selling right next to competition. Find a need and fill it. Make the rounds of stores and flea markets for ideas. Sell a product or a service that will be paid for in cash and immediately. When you live in an RV, you must think of the size and weight of merchandise and equipment. And when you determine the selling price of a product or service, be certain to include all your costs: do not forget the wear on your car and the gas you spend driving to wholesalers or customers. At the maximum, invest only $100 (that you can afford to lose) in something that will replace itself many times and quickly. Do not start big: better pay a bit more for a small quantity until you are very sure of repeat business. Do not give up until you have investigated all the ways to sell a service or a product you like.

If you plan to stay in an area for a while, you can find work through a local newspaper as well as an employment office. You can always apply to a temporary work agency. A nationwide one can transmit your work records from city to city so that benefits can accumulate. Remember to wear business attire when applying for a job and keep copies of your resume available in your RV.

There is a super job, according to Frank and Mary: apply at Disney World! They need people part-time and full-time for their gift shops. These positions are especially advantageous if you have children and grandchildren; they get free use of the park. Many RVers spend their summers working in resorts, children's summer camps and national parks where they can enjoy the spectacular surroundings. They really enjoy being around kids again. Others prefer a work environment for a change and would rather work in a hotel.

Perhaps you have other suggestions. I would appreciate hearing from you, so I can share them in my next book. Please send them to:

Rollanda Masse
FMCA #41126

P.O. Box 44209
Cincinnatti, OH 45244

Important Foreign Country Rules

If you plan to work in a foreign country, you must inquire at its consulate office about possible restrictions that may apply to you. Ask if you need a passport or visa to enter the country. Also, inquire at its customs office about what you are allowed to take with you into the country. And check with your own country's customs office about what you are not allowed to bring back home. Beware, the rules may have changed since the last time you left the country.

Handicapped or Sick

Bill and Nancy are members of the SKP club; Bill had been in business for twenty-five years in California when in 1976 he had a heart attack followed by two operations. At forty-six, he was forced to retire. He decided to return to what he was doing before he married, that is, singing and playing Western music. He started writing his own lyrics and guitar music. His wife Nancy, who sings well, learned to play the bass.

Now they are an excellent duo and play wherever their travels or engagements take them. When they play impromtu at a campground, they just pass the hat. Even after having been very sick, Bill has succeeded in finding a better life, one in which he and his wife are doing what they enjoy: traveling and singing!

Pete Moore, sixty-three, a former machinist and mechanic, sold his house in Albuquerque in 1982. He lives as a nomad on interest from his capital plus a disability pension. He was forced to retire when he hurt his spine in 1976. Often he is unable to stand, so uses a wheelchair much of the time.

Peter is a member of the FMCA club, and its Achievers

International chapter. The function of this organization is to find the most convenient location for the handicapped attending a rally. When he first started traveling he bought a truck-camper, followed by a motorhome, a fifth wheel, and now he owns a thirty-three foot motorhome with which he pulls a Subaru. Peter is a busy person, helping everyone. He is the president of the FMCA Single International Chapter.

In 1973, five handicapped couples from California and Texas decided to travel together for awhile. They found the togetherness such a morale booster and the exchange of information and help so precious that they founded a club: the Handicapped Travel Club, Inc.

Last winter, in Carlsbad, NM, during the Escapade of the SKP Club, I talked briefly with a man in his late sixties whom I had seen walking very slowly. He told me that he had been sick for the last three years. He had lost a lung because of cancer, and had recently had bypass surgery after a heart attack had paralyzed him for awhile. "But I am much better now," he said. "At least I am walking! I am so glad we sold our house. Now we do not have to worry about it. All we have to do, my wife and I, is travel and see our family and friends. We are very lucky that we could come here to attend the Escapade and see all our member friends once more!"

Bob and Lil White make a good pair. Even though he has no legs, Bob drives their motorhome; Lil is the navigator. Since 1975, they have lived and traveled in a motorhome. Bob repairs the RV himself, with Lil's help. He even fixes his friends' RVs sometimes. He says it's easier to work on the engines without legs in the way. He said, "I made a pact with my wife; I will not step on her feet if she does not step on mine. What makes you handicapped is not the loss of your legs; it's the loss of your courage."

Many companies custom build RVs for the handicapped. Some adapt them; others sell accessories for them.

Parents and Young Children

There are some families that travel with children who earn educational credits by mail and are taught by their parents, under the supervision of the authorities. Most people are strongly opposed to this. Some, because they can not imagine themselves teaching their kids; others, because they believe that living fulltime in an RV with children would be too crowded. But the majority think that schooling through correspondence courses will probably not provide an adequate education and the life of a nomad will deprive children of being part of a certain milieu, having a normal social life with their peer group.

From what I have read and heard on the subject, teachers, psychologists and social workers do not agree among themselves on the subject. Some authorities view the traveling experience as a positive complement to the traditional educational experience, and the schooling of these children as being superior. As for the constant changing of environment and friends, some view it as a positive input to the development of personality.

I remember a young couple I met at Key Largo, in Florida, about six years ago. They had sold everything: a business, big house, luxury boat, and had moved into an apartment, and took to the road in a van with their ten-year-old son. When I met them, they had been traveling several months, each parent acting as teacher every second day. They were following a program given to them by a school, and all was well.

Can you imagine the attention this boy received when he talked of the places he had been with other campers, mostly grandparents who missed their own grandchildren? Almost everyone was eager to explain or show something to this beautiful boy who had a charming personality.

His parents told me that previously business and social life had been taking all their time, while their marriage was going to pieces. They decided to change their priorities and try togetherness. . . . and it was working. They said love had come back into their life and they were happy again. They looked radiant, and the kid too.

Pet Owners

RV magazines often feature articles in which writers relate how dogs have been good and not caused any trouble during three months travel from Fairbanks to Panama. Unfortunately, no one even thinks of interviewing Fido!

Life in an RV is one thing for a person, and sometimes quite a different thing for a pet. For instance, many cats become seasick in a moving vehicle; some are terrified. I read of a dog that fell into the canal in front of the lot where his master had parked an RV. There was no way for the dog to climb out and he was almost exhausted when a man in a canoe picked him up. Each year, many pets, not as lucky, die this way, according to this newspaper.

Everywhere, you hear dogs that are left alone in RVs, wailing from fear or loneliness, or barking because of anger and frustration. I have often seen dogs and cats tied outside RVs without shade and water, while their masters have gone shopping or were swimming and lying on the beach. In addition to suffering from heat, these animals can be kicked by passersby or stolen.

Many campgrounds do not even accept pets or, if they do and your dog barks, neighboring campers may become quite annoyed with you. If in spite of the inconveniences and the possible problems, you still want to travel with a pet, here are a few tips:

- Give your pet a chance to get used to traveling by making short trips at first.
- Almost everywhere, you must keep a pet on a leash, so make sure you always carry one.

- During a trip, stop every three hours and let a dog run or at least walk. Dogs need exercise, and drivers deserve rest.
- Always carry little plastic bags with you. Put your hand inside the bag, pick up "the gift" left by your pet, turn the bag inside out and throw it in the trash can. A clean way to handle the mess!
- Before you leave home, take your pet to a veterinarian for shots and necessary treatments for tropical climates.

Occasional Users

Some RVers use their vehicles for weekends only to break the routine and get away from the city noise. They may camp where there are no services, but little do they care! With a modern recreational vehicle, they have their own water and their own heating, cooking and toilet facilities. Or they might park in a campground with all the services, on their own, or as participants in one of the many rallies of dozens of camping clubs.

Others use their own recreational vehicles or ones they have rented for vacations only. They want to be free of the line-ups at the airports and hotel desks. They do not want to have to make do with just any motel or any restaurant when they drive into a town too late to be choosey. They want to be free to eat "at home" in the comfort of their RVs and in the surroundings they choose. There is no need to pack and unpack, no need to change clothes to suit a hotel code— shorts, bathing suits, sweaters and pants are about all they need, unless they decide to go to a fancy restaurant. Vacationing in an RV lets them modify schedules and itineraries as often as they please and helps them save on hotel and restaurant bills.

Some people travel in RVs only a few months a year. Others use them only to go from a house up north to a house down south, and maybe for a few trips now and then. Some people use RVs for work, like the traveling salesman who uses his RV as a showroom, or the performer whose RV becomes his dressing room. Some municipalities use large RVs as mobile libraries. And the Red Cross is not the only organization that uses RVs as mobile clinics; a California dentist uses his RV to make house calls!

CHAPTER 2

What Do You Call These Houses on Wheels?

Statistics and History

Today there are approximately 61 million Americans who camp, and according to A.C. Nielson, that number is expected to be 64.4 million in 1990. Not everyone who camps likes tenting; many prefer houses on wheels called recreational vehicles (RVs).

The 1989 figures published by the Recreational Vehicle Industry Association (RVIA) show that 25 million Americans are camping in RVs. The American Association of Retired Persons (AARP) estimates that 9 million senior Americans use RVs on an annual basis.

Why are RVs so popular? They provide travelers with the most economical means of transportation by rolling travel, lodging and dining into one practical package and doing it in comfort and style. And, there is no better way to forget about the rest of the world than to go off camping.

We've all seen movies showing the early settlers traveling across America with their homes, rudimentary covered wagons containing all of their belongings. They must have had a great sense of adventure and this is perhaps the same drive that inspires modern RV travelers. Of course, their life does not depend on getting to their destinations, but they are curious to see what's ahead, and they like the convenience of having their homes with them, while they wander across the country.

When the first car was invented, there were people who wanted to take off for a trip right away in the marvelous machine. Already in 1915, Henry Ford was going to the mountains with a truck containing all his equipment. In 1935, he bought a trailer with electricity; it contained a stove, an ice box, a sink, a toilet, some cabinets and two convertible beds. He loaned this trailer to Lindberg who used it to tour the province of Ontario and 39 states.

In 1926, George Barnes owned a skillfully built home-designed "housecar." At that time, the mere sight of a truck with a "live-in house" on it was a rarity; seeing one that was self-contained was unheard of. When George parked his home on wheels on the streets of Los Angeles, people lined up just to have a look.

RV Economics

RV camping vacations are the most economical type of vacation in the U.S., according to a summer 1987 study by Pannell Kerr Forster. This is regardless of the type of RV used, trip distance, trip duration or region of the country. The hypothetical travel party was a family of four. For a period of fourteen nights, vacationing with a trailer and a light-duty truck, the estimated cost was $1,253, compared to $2,548 in a car and sleeping in motels or hotels. It was $3,524 in a train and motels or hotels, and $4,118 for airfare, motels or hotels. Thats about 3¼ times more than camping.

If after reading this book, you decide you would like to buy an RV, using the above comparisons, you will be able to estimate how much you will save on your future vacations. Granted, you will have to buy the RV, but this money invested will not disappear! You will always have the RV's market value to add to your financial statement. And you'll always have the enjoyment and the convenience of owning it, whether for a month's vacation or an overnight trip. And, it will always be there should you decide to become a nomad.

Names

People in any way involved with the RVs, do not always agree about the proper terms to use when discussing the vehicles. Strangers to RVing often call my mini-motorhome a camper, a truck, a trailer, a Winnebago or a mobile home. Well, if mobile homes are in the RV category, they are surely the largest; they measure thirty to seventy feet long by ten to twenty-six feet wide, and contain the same plumbing systems, appliances and furniture found in an ordinary house. If it is an RV, it surely becomes the least mobile of them all, once a screened porch is attached to it and a "skirt" is added around its base to hide its wheels or hide the fact that its wheels have been removed. It is often called a manufactured home. New, it may cost from $20,000 to $75,000, depending on the unit, the park where it is located and whether the lot is included in the price. Most of the time, in parks, the lot is only rented. *(All RV measurements and prices are approximate.)*

The *park model,* also called a *park trailer* is ordinarily included with the RVs. Although it often comes with self-contained facilities and can be used like a travel trailer, the majority of the new ones are similar to the mobile homes; the appointments resemble those of an ordinary house. They are used in campgrounds where the zoning prohibits mobile homes. They can measure ten to fourteen feet wide by thirty to forty-seven feet long. New, they cost between $10,000 to $48,000, depending on location and if the lot is included.

For people who do not want to travel, these two types of units become an attractive alternative to a regular house. Both are easier to maintain and cheaper to buy. When located in a well-appointed park with swimming pool, spa, recreation hall and planned activities, they offer a pleasant community life.

Towables that travel are:

- the folding camping trailer, the least expensive but also the least practical for the nomad life
- the travel trailer, which measures thirteen to twenty-six feet and costs new $4,000 to $49,000
- the fifth-wheel travel trailer, nineteen to forty feet and costing new $8,000 to $50,000

The motorized RVs are:

- the truck camper also called pick-up camper (the camper is actually the camping-equipped unit loaded on the bed of the pick-up), which measures six to twelve feet and costs new $3,000 to $13,000 (without truck)
- the van conversion, fifteen to twenty-one feet and costing new $18,000 to $39,000
- the mini-motorhome and micro-mini, seventeen to twenty-nine feet and costing new $21,000 to $60,000
- the motorhomes and busses, twenty-four to forty feet and costing new $31,000 to $600,000 and more

Above are the main RV categories. To learn more about their individual features, buy a *RV Buyer Guide* that shows details of all the models and all the dozens of different layouts. Attending RV shows is also a good way to see many models and, of course, visiting RV dealers' lots will help you get answers to your questions.

For first-time RVers and for people with a low budget, a used RV is a good choice. It is possible to get a good, not very old, twenty-one foot travel trailer for about $3,000. To tow it, find a good second-hand big car.

RV Facilities

Except for some small trailers, vans and campers, RVs have toilets and showers (some even have whirlpools). RVs are equipped with a fresh water tank and one or two holding tanks for "gray" water from the sinks and shower and for "black" water from the toilet. These tanks are easily connected to a campground sewer outlet to give the same service as that of a house. An unlimited supply of water is available when you can connect the RV hose to a campground or a house water outlet.

Generally, the refrigerator works on propane, on 12 volts (the same current you have for your radio in your car) or on 110 volts (the same as house current). The stove also works on propane, as do the water heater and the furnace. But the fan of the furnace needs electric power; it operates on 12 volts, as does the lighting. The current source is the car battery or/and an RV or marine battery installed in the RV. When connected to a campground or a house outlet, the unit functions on 110 volts just as a regular house. Then you can use a computer, a microwave oven, a regular toaster, etc.

Boondocking

However, if you want to be really independent and still be able to use any appliance wherever you park without connections (it's called boondocking), you could get a generator, an inverter or some solar panels. Then you would have 110v wherever you park. As for the accumulation of gray and black waters, you can connect your sewer hose to a portable tank that you empty at dumping stations, found at all campgrounds, most RV dealers, some rest areas, some truck stops and at some rental truck agencies where they repair RVs.

Depending on how long you plan to stay in that beautiful secluded spot where you'll get peace and quiet in communion with nature, you might want to bring extra fresh water in jugs. You will have to rely on a few boondocking tricks, some of which you probably have heard from nature conservationists. You can live without a daily shower; our grandparents did because most of them did not have the facilities. It is possible to take a sponge bath with a washcloth, and be clean and save a lot of water. You don't keep the water running while you do it. Ditto for when you brush your teeth, wash the dishes, etc. For even greater water savings, you can use this gray water to flush the toilet.

When you refill your fresh water tank at a gas station or elsewhere, make sure it is fresh potable water. It is smart to use your own RV hose since garden hoses usually give a bad taste, and may not be sanitary. They probably have been used for filling radiators, etc.

You can find propane at some gas stations, truck stops, truck rental agencies, RV dealers and campgrounds. Your tank or tanks should be carried in an open compartment and standing up. Be sure you turn off every appliance and the main tank valve before refilling your propane tanks. The same precaution is advised when you stop for gasoline along the road.

Auxiliary Transportation

The majority of RVers living in a motorhome pull a car. Some boating enthusiasts carry a small boat, on top of a towed car. Many tow a boat instead of a car. But what if you would like to have use of a large boat? Investigate the Camp-A-Float facilities, where you drive your RV on a motorized raft and cast off. You are off on a cruise in your own "instant" houseboat with no suitcase to pack!

For someone who wants a car along, but hates to tow it, the solution is the Cloud Liner, a luxury thirty-eight-foot motorhome with a small car garage under the elevated back bedroom.

One of the drawbacks of traveling with a travel trailer is that you cannot tow anything but the trailer. You can always carry a small boat on top of the towing vehicle but many people would like to enjoy a larger boat. A couple once parked a truck beside me that was pulling a platform on which there was a small houseboat. These clever campers were at home everywhere, even on the water.

Some RVers tow impressive motorcycles on trailers; others prefer to carry light and less expensive scooters and mopeds on bumper racks. By far the greater number of RVers carry bicycles in the back or in the front, where they get less dirty. Some RVers prefer the folding ones with 20-inch wheels. They are practical; even folding tricycles fit in the large rooftop pods. And, you must see the new four-wheel two-person cycling arrangement! Whatever kind of auxiliary transportation you use, remember to tie down everything with chains and padlocks, but make sure no one can steal the whole rack or trailer.

CHAPTER 3

Where Do You Park Overnight?

When I tell people I live and travel year round in my mini-motorhome, they always ask: "Where is your home?" My answer is what the Escapees Club members use: "Home is where I park it." Then they ask where I park overnight and my answer is: "In any state or province." At one time or another, I have parked in every kind of place.

Government Parks

If the place where you really would like to camp is in the middle of awesome scenery, national parks and forests and most of the state parks should be your first choice. If you select campsites without hook-ups (utility connections), you might pay only $2 a night. (*All campground fees are approximate.*) If you decide to boondock for a few weeks, not only will you save on camping fees (*if* they are less than commercial campgrounds), but you will also save on gas by staying put for a while. This is the way many fulltimers replenish their wallet, so they can keep traveling on a modest budget.

Someone once conveyed to me the joy of boondocking as follows: "We'd arrived at Coconico National Forest, north of Flagstaff, and parked our RV in the campground. The needles from the overhanging giant pines were falling down on our picnic table. Other RVers had already started a campfire; we joined them and chattered while the sun was going down behind the San Francisco mountains in all its glory of multiple shades of red, orange and yellow. After a while, in this relaxed ambience, we were getting sleepy and as we were saying goodnight, a coyote started to howl; it was just like a call to bed. Everyone laughed and decided it was bedtime. There was no lighting in this camp. There were no stars that night, but total blackness with only the mysterious forest surrounding us. The coyote was silent. This was peace.

"The next morning, we enjoyed our ham and egg breakfast in the majesty of the snow-topped mountains, the highest of Arizona. Then, we set out for the hiking trail amidst the lava beds of the Wupatki National Monument."

For lovers of great expanses of land, of remote lakes and rivers, of endless forests, there are also fabulous spots to park at national monuments and on land managed by the Bureau of Land Management, the U.S. Army Corps of Engineers (COE), the Federal Energy Regulatory Commission, and in some county parks as well as in Canadian national and provincial parks.

According to the brochures, the many Canadian national parks offer the following activities: fishing, boating, hunting, hiking, cross-country skiing and snowshoing, swimming, scuba diving, horseback riding, golf, tennis, mountain climbing, cycling, as well as an opportunity to benefit from exhibits, interpretative programs and exercise trails. Write for details.

Free Overnight Parking Places

Among the natural parks, one of the favorites of Western RVers is the Slabs, which is administered by the Bureau of Land Management. Thousands of RVers spend their winters there. They pay $25 for a permit and then park free. There are many other places like this.

The first time my husband and I used a trailer to go down South was at the beginning of November in 1980. The first evening we ended up somewhere in Kentucky. Using a directory, we selected a campground supposedly six miles distant from the highway. In reality, it was ten miles and down a very narrow road where we turned, went up and down, and turned again and again before finally arriving at a nice campground on a lake.

After it snowed most of the night, these ten miles back over a slippery, narrow, twisting road, were very scary and seemed extra long to us the next morning. Many times since, we have left the highway to look for a campground that was easily found and very comfortable, but many other times, after a long search, we had to park on a site that was muddy and uneven. And all we were using was the electric hook-up for the TV. We didn't bother to connect the water or the sewer just for the night.

I now have a TV that works on 12 volts (the car lighter). I am not spending $10, 15 or 20 any more for only a place to sleep overnight. I use campgrounds and pay happily, only if I need the services provided, like connections for the 110 volt current, for drinking water and sewer. I may swim in the pool, use the laundry, and perhaps participate in all the activities offered. That makes it worthwhile to pay the fees for a few days or more.

Now on my own, I still follow the procedure my husband and I found worked best. When we thought it was time to stop, we watched for signs of truck stops with restaurants open 24 hours. They usually are advertised far ahead of time and most are well kept places. It is so easy to park in them. No need to drive miles on unknown roads; they are right on the side of the highway and the ground is level. We park near the lighted restaurant, being careful not to be in the way of the other customers and of trucks. There are other RVs and much going on, so nobody pays attention to me. Of course, I do not turn the radio on full blast or take the chairs out. I keep quiet. To shut out the noise of the trucks, I use the pink wax ear plugs sold in drugstores and sleep soundly in my little mobile hotel. In the morning, I may have breakfast in the restaurant and/or buy some groceries, postcards and newspapers. I get gas and am back on the road easily. Very simple . . . and you can't beat the price!

Boondocking is nothing new for experienced RVers. It's been done for years. It helps twentieth century nomads with modest incomes cope with the high cost of living. But mind you, there are many RVers with enough money to pay for campgrounds all the time, who are boondocking too. They prefer the freedom of stopping when and where they please. Why not use the self-sufficiency of an RV? You have paid good money for a modern home on wheels with all the necessary systems. Their real advantage is the ability they provide to be free to spend a few days in a quiet, isolated area by a river, or in a majestic forest, or anywhere that appeals or is convenient.

Friends of mine told me that when they buy produce from farmers, they often ask permission to park on the property. One time a farmer invited them to tour the farm and have dinner with his family. The next day, the farmers "toured" the motorhome and had lunch. Like millions of others, they had never been in an RV. My friends ended up spending three days on this farm!

There are numerous places where you can park free for one night and sometimes for a few days. Here are some suggestions from the nomads:

- farms
- truck stops
- shopping centers, under a light, in front of a store that is open all night
- rest areas, which are lighted and spacious enough for semi-trailers (these drivers need to rest somewhere . . . try not to be in their way); rest areas that provide tourist information often provide water and a dumping station
- closed truck weighing stations; again, leave space for the truckers
- wide vacant spaces near the entrance of a highway, where the equipment was stored during construction.
- sand or gravel excavation sites; park out of the way
- historical markers; there is usually room for only one RV
- scenic lookouts
- service stations; if you see space, gas up and ask permission
- bank parking lots; stay away from the building and the police patrol car's path around the building
- church parking lots; ask for permission.
- lodge parking, such as Kiwanis or Moose; ask permission if someone is there; they sometimes have water and electrical outlets
- out-of-business stores and service stations
- convenience stores, if the parking area is exceptionally large; buy something and ask permission.
- laundromats, sometimes open all night; always park away from the entrance
- parking lots of closed medical clinics
- cinema parking
- police stations, if they have large parking areas; ask, and if they refuse, they might suggest another free spot, that they know will be secure
- fire houses
- post offices, if they have large parking lots, are very handy if that's where you'll pick up your mail

- restaurants; ask the waitress while you're eating; she will get her boss to agree since she hopes for a big tip
- K-Mart lots; their headquarters has announced that RVers are welcome to park overnight in this favorite "campground chain" of the nomads; you most probably will not be alone
- RV dealers; you might buy an accessory or something else and ask permission; they often have a dumping station
- various tourist attractions; Sea World, in San Diego, CA, welcomes overnight RVers
- vacant building sites or vacant lots; pick up some cans, trash, etc., and put it in a bag that you leave by your RV; if someone questions you, show that you help instead of harming and you'll get permission for staying as long as you want

Anymore ideas are welcome. So that I can share them in my next book, please send them to:

Rollanda D. Masse,
FMCA # 41126,
P.O. Box 44209,
Cincinnatti, OH 45244

This list is far from complete, you will surely find many other spots.

Be sure to keep a good reputation as an RVer. Treat every place where you park like your own garden and do not empty garbage cans, ashtrays and, above all holding tanks in inappropriate places. I just heard about a shopping center, a longtime favorite place of RVers, that is now off limits after business hours because of inconsiderate emptying of holding tanks, and now the reputation of all RVers is hurt again, because of a few.

Wherever you park, always make sure that you are not in

the way of residents, employees, clients and cars the next morning. Ask yourself, "will I be in someone's way?" Always be fair and considerate and do not take space where there is little parking, and always try to buy something from the stores where you park.

If you're going to boondock, about one hour before you want to stop, start looking for that free spot. You'll be amazed at how many places there are. If you don't like what is available at the time you want to stop, you can always return to one of the places you've spotted earlier. But, this won't be necessary when you've become an expert. I do recommend one thing: stop before it gets dark. If you should have an emergency on the road, being stranded at night will make the situation more difficult.

The Fears

The first time you boondock, you may be very nervous. You'll probably jump at every noise. You will think every car driving by is someone coming to chase you away. You may still be nervous the second and the third time; at least, my husband and I were. But, after a few experiences, it will all be matter of fact and you will wonder why you have not stopped paying campground fees before.

In talking with other nomads, I have realized that the main reason some RVers do not boondock is that they are afraid someone will come and chase them away in the middle of the night. Well, it has never happened to me in eight years. Once, in a shopping center in Leesburg, Florida, a policeman knocked on the door at nine o'clock in the evening. He apologized for disturbing us, asked if we planned to spend the night there, and explained that the owners did not allow parking overnight, but if we would go one mile down the road, there was a K-Mart where we'd probably find other RVs. All of this he said, very politely.

The same thing happened to us in White City, New Mexico, a place with several attractions and a few bars. We parked in front of a nice restaurant where we had dined. There was only a small parking lot, and we should have asked permission. A man in uniform asked us politely to leave and directed us to the nearest campground, which seemed to be affiliated with the restaurant.

Another time, I had stopped for the night on a hospital parking lot in Ontario. Around 9:30, a lady in uniform came and asked me if my husband was in the hospital. Before I could answer she said, "Sleep peacefully, I am making the rounds and I am watching."

We heard a similar expression of caring from two policemen on patrol in a shopping center when we were parked near the K-Mart garage where we had an early appointment the next morning.

Only four times in eight years have I been approached, and always with polite questions. And I have parked hundreds of times overnight in assorted locations.

According to the National Council on Crime and Delinquency, most hold-ups and thefts need planning and occur in banks, service stations, liquor stores and unoccupied residences. Studying National Council figures, a statistician estimated there was only one chance in a million that a theft would take place in an RV and only one in 30 millions that an RVer would be murdered.

Considering all the thefts and murders committed in regular houses, it seems odd that RVers, who are not scared to sleep in a house or in an apartment where the majority of crimes occur, are afraid to sleep in a lighted spot, most of the time near other RVs. Why would anyone try to force entry into an RV parked in full light to find, in all probability, only a small TV, a camera and some travelers' checks? With the curtains drawn, who knows how many people could be inside?

Like most nomads, I am very prudent. I weigh the chances of an accident's happening. I don't park anywhere I have not surveyed first. If an area is dilapidated and seems to be a questionable neighborhood, I keep going. Personally, I prefer to stay overnight in a well-lit place where there are comings and goings. I park so the front of my RV is facing outwards. This way I can leave any premises rapidly, and if I happen to have left my lights on (I've done that twice), someone can get to the battery and charge it with the booster cables I carry.

I know a dog is the best guardian; I don't know how many people kindly have suggested I get one! So, when I stop for the night in a shopping center, for instance, I take out a large dog food bowl with some water, fix a big chain to the RV entrance handle, and put my "Beware of Dog" sign in the window. Who would dare to come near? And I have no dog to scold, feed, walk, brush and take to the veterinarian. "My dog" costs me no money. And when I want to spend a week at a friend's cabin, or three days in a luxury hotel in Mexico City, as I did last winter, I have no dog sitting problems.

There is a cassette of dog barking that you can order from Camping World, and RV dealers sell all kinds of alarm system. But, remember, your RV is a fortress as long as you're inside. Do not open the door without checking who's there. A policeman will stand under the light so you'll see his uniform. If your name is written outside, as on many RVs, beware that anyone can call you by name to try to catch you off guard. When you leave your RV, you should close the drapes and leave the lights and the radio on, so that a prowler will think someone is home.

Do not advertise your RV as your residence, on a bumper sticker for instance. A thief may be more tempted, thinking you probably have valuables since you're not simply a vacationer.

Since I have been alone, I do not affix my singles club logos to my RV. I display a man's hat and a big "#1 GRANDPA" coffee mug on the dashboard. When filling up in a gas station, if I feel uncomfortable, I pretend to talk to a husband who has stayed inside behind a closed curtain. Only once have I actually resorted to this comedy and it was mostly for practice. By being ready and by being prudent, even though you are alone, you can take advantage of all the free parking places.

I remember the Darlingtons who came to talk to us and with whom we had lunch at Fort Myers Beach; they are SKPs and had spotted the Escapees sticker on our motorhome. When we asked where they were camping, they told us they were right on the beach! They were walking the beach when they spotted a construction site; as experienced nomads, they saw an opportunity to camp free. They talked with the person in charge, who was glad to have an RV on the site as a deterrent to vandalism. So, our SKP friends were set up with water and electricity, use of the building's toilets, and even a phone was brought into their motorhome. They spent two months there, they told me when I met them later in Texas. Only once did they have to call the police, and when the four young prowlers heard the siren, they took off in a flash. Two months at the same place was a record for these fulltime nomads. But, two months directly on the beach is a dream of many people. And to think that it was free!

Commercial Campgrounds

There are approximately 12,000 commercial campgrounds in the U.S. That includes the condo ones, but the vast majority are campgrounds where you cannot buy a lot. They might rent from $6 to $36 daily, depending on what they offer and above all, where they are situated. Some give you only water and electric hook-ups, no showers, no laundry facilities and may be far from local attractions. And there are also the extra large, super deluxe accommodations, like Indian Creek Park in Fort Myers, Florida, Golden Village at Hemet, California, the Voyager RV Resort in Tucson, Arizona. The Tropic Star in

Pharr, Texas boasts a large swimming pool, nine-hole golf course, tennis courts, huge dance hall, billiard rooms, and five or six large rooms for hobbies like ceramics, art, sewing (machines supplied), bridge and poker. Organized activities include the following: four kinds of exercise classes every morning, yoga, square dancing, horseshoes, woodworking, shuffleboard, ceramics, knitting, bridge, line dancing, Spanish dancing, cribbage and pinochle, round dancing, and that's the program for Friday only! If RVers still have time to look at TV, there is a tv cable jack as well as the telephone jack at the site.

Fees in well organized campgrounds are around $16 to $36 a night and about $300 to $700 monthly. Weekly rates are comparable. As a rule, it is less expensive in Texas and Arizona camps than in those in Florida or California. They all have special deals for five- or six-month stays and will store RVs on campsites or in a storage area. Some parks even have trailers for rent.

A nice and inexpensive way to live for someone who does not want to travel anymore is to return to the same campground in the South year after year. You spend winters with the same old friends and live a similar worry-free way during the summer in a well-appointed campground up north.

KOA Campgrounds

Many traveling RVers use KOA campgrounds almost exclusively. They travel with a KOA directory and KOA 10% discount card. (FMCA gives one to its members). Most KOAs are very well kept, and many are located near large cities and offer city tours. In Montreal, Canada, Montreal South KOA is an excellent campground, which offers bus tours as well as information to tour on your own. They will make reservations for you at the Quebec City KOA, which also offers tours and the same welcome. In fact, all KOAs make reservations for their customers at other KOAs. Some also have "kabins" for rent.

Campgrounds for Members Only

The Camper Ranch Club of America owns eight camps in Arizona, Oklahoma, Texas and New Mexico; one has a swimming pool, all have recreation halls and many acres in the natural state. To become a life member costs $1,600 plus a $75 annual fee. For that you can camp as often and as long as you want in any of them.

There are campgrounds where the owners of Airstream trailers can buy a lot for about $7,000. The Loners on Wheels Club has two campgrounds with lots for about the same price. The Escapees (SKPs) Club now has about twenty co-op campgrounds and retreats and more being developed. There is one with pool in Florida that sells lots for $6,500 and another in Texas that sells lots for $2,500. In all of these parks, an owner, who is not occupying his lot, can ask the manager to rent it for him. If someone wishes to sell a lot, it is offered to the first member on the waiting list at a stable price. An owner makes no profit but he is certain of selling with no loss of money. Due to the fixed prices, there is always a waiting list in the SKP's camps.

Membership Campground Chains

There are three or four chains of membership campgrounds, but the most stable and the most important is Camp Coast-to-Coast (CCC). This chain adds to its organization already established high quality campgrounds. The owner of these newly integrated parks offers membership cards that cost from $2,000 to more than $10,000 with $200 and up annual fees. RVers may camp for no additional fee for fourteen days in a row. They must then depart for at least seven days before being able to camp for fourteen days again, and so on for as often as they wish. There can be variations on this.

Once you are a member of this park organization, you can camp at any other of the 500 parks in Canada and the U.S. for $1 a day, with a limit of two seven-day stays in the same park in one year. There are other advantages, such as RV insurance and services similar to those offered to camping club members. Most of these campgrounds do not accept nonmembers, only the 375,000 CCC members.

There are obvious advantages to this membership, but many nomads do not like to have to reserve thirty days, very often sixty days, ahead of time. It kills the pleasure of stopping at will. In high season, it's almost impossible to gain access to these campgrounds. Most of them are located many miles away from main highways and it's not worth it to use the gas and the time just to pay only $1 to camp overnight. On a holiday weekend, many parks will accept only their own park members. If a park does not conform to the regulations or, for any reason, is removed from the chain, the members lose.

However, many fulltimers use these parks a lot when they want to stay put for a while and save money. While staying put and saving on gas, they meet other fulltimers doing the same thing. It's like a club; you meet the same people wherever you go. So, you have to decide if it is worth it to invest thousands of dollars (it's not easy to sell these memberships; you may lose money). In addition, remember the annual fees. Although most members travel with their reservations written on a calendar, some just drop in and take their chances. They say they are welcome most of the time, especially during quiet periods.

You would be wise to inquire at more than one site to learn all the aspects of each contract, legal and otherwise. You can also purchase a "secondhand" membership through any of the many brokers advertised in the club magazines.

Condominium Campgrounds

Buying a condo lot can be advantageous for the RVer who is making plans for the day when he will want to stay put. He can rent it while he travels (the management looks after arrangements) and stop there once in a while to make friends for the later years.

Buying a condo lot is like buying a condo apartment; if you buy one before or during construction and if it is well located and well designed, you are probably going to make money if you sell it when the park is finished and other lots are occupied. To give a general idea of price, in Florida, "bare bones" campgrounds in the middle of nowhere probably don't sell their lots for much less than $10,000.

Among the most luxurious is the Outdoor Resorts of America chain where members of FMCA get a 10% discount. The one at Melbourne Beach in Florida is located between the Atlantic Ocean and Indian River on the Intercoastal Waterway. There is a beach on the seaside and a flower-tiled swimming pool. RVers situated on the riverfront can dock their boats right in front of their lots. On this side there is a long fishing pier with a charming covered deck at the end and a beautiful large recreational hall and huge swimming pool, with plenty of room for pool parties. Although there are only five hundred sites, there is another pool with an exercise room and sauna and another recreational room in the center of the camp. A convenience store is located close to the entrance. All this is surrounded with luxuriant landscaping, including twisting paths and a bridge over the small cascades.

The daily rent is bout $30 and the lots sell between $40,000 to $80,000 now, depending on location. At this writing, there is one resale lot in the Palm Spring Resorts in California advertised at $81,000, which backs up to the golf course. Presently, a new condo campground near Key West, Blue Water Key, sells lots starting at $52,500.

Special Interest Campgrounds

Although the clientele is mixed in most campgrounds some cater to people with the same interest. Examples include the River Ranch of the Outdoor Resort of America chain, located at Lake Wales in Florida. Here you can live Western style and enjoy horseback riding, square dancing, and Western music concerts. At Will Mettan's nudist park in Springfield, Oregon, you camp in the nude or dressed. The Clerbrook RV Resort at Clermont, Florida, includes a complete golf course in the list of its facilities.

Five hydro pools are part of the equipment of the Fountain of Youth Spa and RV Park in Niland, California. Horseworld in Scottsdale, Arizona, is an equestrian center with polo matches, rodeos and dog shows. There are hundreds more campgrounds that offer special interest facilities and activities. You can find them by checking campground directories, the Tourism Bureaux, camping club news letters and RV magazines and newspapers.

City Campgrounds

A few commercial campgrounds are located right in cities and there are some cities that have municipal campgrounds. Generally, these campgrounds offer only basic facilities, sometimes a pool. But they are so well located that it is worth the trouble to find them. San Francisco has one and New Orleans has several commercial campgrounds, in front of which you can board a city bus to do your own exploring. Tour buses also pick up campers right in the parks.

Another one that is practical is the Shoreline RV Park in downtown Long Beach, California. It is close to the old liner *Queen Mary* and the huge plane *Spruce Goose*, built by Howard Hughes.

While a Good Sam member was getting treatments at the Mayo Clinic, she lived in an RV at the Silver Lake Trailer Park in Rochester, Minnesota, and promptly fell in love with its campground. Now in good health, she still camps there. Her neighbors during her first stay had been sick too, and, like her, they have come back again and again. They all enjoy the quiet scenery along the Zumbro River. Some come to fish, others to shop in the classy stores (where they sometimes encounter a celebrity), or to dine in the Rochester restaurants. *Ann* likes especially Le Bistro, which she describes as: "A charming French café, all decorated in pink like a bonbon and surrounded by all kinds of fancy boutiques." Silver Lake is a waterfront campground in a country setting close to beautiful stores and eating places of a city. It seems to me to be the best of two worlds!

CHAPTER 4

Where Do You Travel?

Fulltime wanderers in houses on wheels have the advantage of traveling when they want and where they want, while most people live in one place and travel only during their annual vacations. Those in the second group might want to consider taking time off for a year or two or retiring early. They could find out what it's like to live and roam about as they please for a change.

Anyone who becomes a nomad, even temporarily, can find adventure somewhere—be it panning the water of Colorado rivers in search of gold flakes, catching tuna in the Gulf of Mexico, celebrating Mardi Gras in New Orleans or camping in the panoramic splendor of Utah.

Most fulltime nomads spend the winters where it's warm and the summers far from the heat of the deserts and the humidity of the tropics. Usually in November most fulltimers head for the South, some to Mexico, but most to the Southern states. Some travel extensively throughout one state during six months. Many are members of the different clubs I will describe, and plan their traveling so they can attend club rallies. I do that and I wander from state to state, trying to see and experience everything I can. I believe that it is better not to make any fixed plans. I always find something interesting and want to prolong my stay and make unforeseen detours. Such is the (very agreeable, thank you) life of the nomad at heart!

Tours Organized for RVers

I have joined four organized tours for RVs; each time I came back enchanted and very glad to have paid a little more than if I had made the trip on my own. First, it was a treat for me not to have to plan a trip and the itineraries, stops, mileage, reservations and schedules. (mission impossible!) Yes, it's a relief to put the maps and pamphlets aside and rely on a leader while enjoying the good company of a group of compatible people.

Moreover, we went to the best restaurants and saw places I would probably have missed on my own; perhaps I would not have known about them or I would have arrived too late. I have enjoyed a number of shows, demonstrations, cocktail parties and visits only offered to groups. Sometimes we traveled in private vans to locations with difficult access, and most of the time we had a guide assigned to our group, who was anxious to hear our comments and answer our questions.

In Mexico, the security of being in a group with your own mechanic is invaluable. And the sense of friendship that permeates these groups is a pleasure. After a few days of sharing experiences and impressions, you feel as though you are part of a family. I still see, from time to time, wonderful people I met in a 1980 caravan.

Several companies and camping clubs organize trips that function in a variety of ways: RVers may meet in a campground and travel in their own vehicles, following each other some of the time in a caravan. They may leave their RVs in a campground and travel on a bus. They may meet (without

RVs) at an airport and fly overseas where rented RVs await them for individual or group travel. Some companies and clubs that organize RV tours include:

- Tracks to Adventure (Alaska, Quebec and the Maritimes, the Calgary Stampede, Mardi Gras in New Orleans, fall color tours, New Zealand and Australia, Mexico)
- Caravans Voyagers (Mexico, New Zealand and Australia, Spain, Italy, Scandinavia, Alaska, Nova Scotia, Calgary)
- Point South (Mexico and Alaska)
- Creative World Rallies and Caravans (more than twenty tours almost anywhere you want to go)
- FMCA Camping Club (tours for members by Creative World Rallies and Caravans)
- Amigo RV Tours (Mexico, Alaska, Hawaii, Australia, New Zealand and China; members of Escapees Club get a 20% discount)
- Good Sam Club (more than twenty tours and cruises)
- Airstream, Winnebago and other brand name clubs
- Camping Coast to Coast (tours for members)
- Camping World
- Newspaper Camp-Orama
- International Caravaning Association (tours to many places, Russia included)
- Charles Griffith, of Escapees (Mexico and Alaska)
- New Zealand Tours and Alaska Caravan Adventures
- Alaska-Yukon RV Caravans

Traveling in groups with these experts is the best way to see the world and to make new friends.

When traveling in a caravan (one RV behind the other), you must remember to leave enough space in front of you for a bus or a semi-trailer truck. These drivers are rushing; they are on schedules. Sometimes they have to pass the RVs one by one, so give them a break. Passing through a city, remember to be courteous to the residents at peak traffic times and give them a chance to pass and get to work. In a fairly long caravan of seven or more, it's best to stay off the CB channel the leader has chosen to give instructions on, and better to use another channel for comments or conversation with fellow RVers.

Planning Your Own Trips

To plan travel in North America, you need an Atlas road map. To find the zip codes of cities you wish to write to, consult the book at the post office or buy your own book at a bookstore. You will receive dozens of brochures and sometimes discount coupons for restaurants, theme parks, etc. A free and easy way to get all the information you need is to spend a rainy day at a municipal library. You don't have to be a resident to use a public library if you don't take a book out.

When you select a place to visit, consider the best month for your trip. For example, for a visit to the Grand Canyon National Park, summertime is crowded and you are not permitted to tour in an RV. Winter is out, but April is ideal; you can RV around, stop and camp without a problem.

Some regions are more beautiful to see during certain seasons, like the northern states where the trees show multi-colored foliage in the fall and beautiful flowers in the spring. And, did you know that the arid desert is carpeted with beautiful flowers after a spring shower? If you want to use the national and other government parks facilities in season, it's recommended that you check their reservation policies ahead of time.

If a special interest inspires you to become better acquainted with the American Indians, or to collect and polish stones, or to pursue any hobby, consult a library and/or obtain publications that will tell you the best places to go. Magazines of camping clubs often publish articles about different hobbies pursued by RVers.

When planning an itinerary, consider including interesting stops in scenic and historical areas. There are some along the main highways, but many will take you to secondary roads. The slower pace and the many sights along the way will be a welcome change after a few hours of travel. Between Washington and Baltimore, for instance, there is quiet countryside. It's pleasant to wander from one charming country road to another; it's a calming and refreshing experience. In some states, scenic roads are suggested to motorists; for example, the Tennessee Parkway System covers 2,300 miles of a scenic highway that unites the state parks, the important lakes, the historical sites and the recreational areas. The tourist department has installed 2,000 signs that you can follow.

And the roads are not the only objects of interest while traveling. There are also the people you meet! At Frederick, in Maryland, a lady was sitting on her porch, her young grandson on her lap. Everywhere around her, there were wooden animals and toys. There was no "for sale," sign, but when my friend stopped and asked her if the toys were for sale, the lady answered, quite abashed, "Yes, I'll sell you any one you like." She explained that her husband carved them and she painted them. They were beautifully done and she was selling them all for less than $7. Anybody who stopped by not only found a bargain, but also had the chance to chat with this lady who, by her smile and each of her words, expressed a contagious interior serenity.

RVing in Russia and Other Overseas Countries

During the forties, a few Americans shipped their RVs overseas when they planned to tour Europe. However, after the expansion of air cargo, it became very expensive to ship anything by boat. Furthermore, most modern American RVs are so big that they do not fit in narrow European streets. Today it is more convenient to rent smaller RVs to use in foreign countries than to use your own.

Several airline companies provide help in making arrangements to rent an RV in Europe or elsewhere in the world. A competent travel agency will also communicate with such companies as InterRent, Kemwel, Auto-Europe, Europe by Car, Foremost Euro-Car, Europacar Tours and Majellano Tours. Go Vacation has rental RVs in twenty-two North American cities and in forty-one in Europe, Australia and New Zealand.

Many travelers economize by buying a used RV when they arrive in London, take their tours, then, back in London, sell the vehicle to other tourists. The exact spot for these transactions is near Hungerford Bridge. One couple from Ohio made enough to pay for the expenses of one month traveling. According to them, the RVs sold there are perfect; they are old vans from Dutch posts that have been retrofitted by a man from Australia.

For information on camping in Europe, write to the European Travel Commission. The book *Europe Free* explains exactly how to travel in a van in Europe. Get in touch with Caravan Abroad for information on vans, airplane tickets, etc. The book *Best European Tips* is also a help. In Paris, the Valem Company rents a "camping car." Recently, Cruise America announced that its RVs will be available for rent in Canada and Europe. Or you may arrange a trade through the International Camper Exchange, which deals with campers from everywhere.

If you want to RV in Mexico and don't have an RV, Sanborn's Viva Tours will supply a motorhome with a tour. Something new in Mexico is the luxurious Outdoor Resort of America campground in Baha, Ensenada, which has 280 sites on the ocean for sale or rent. For information on Mexico, write to the Mexican Government Tourism Office or Sanborn's Mexican Insurance.

Another way to go is to put your RV aboard the *Stardancer* and cruise to Alaska or Mexico with Admiral Cruise, Inc., or Alaska-Yukon RV Caravans. If you want to camp in Alaska, Mike and Marilyn Miller provide information in their book *Camping Alaska and Canada's Yukon*, 112 pages with photos and maps.

Once you are in Canada's Yukon, if it's spring, you might as well travel across Canada. You could start in Victoria, with its double-decker buses, its old English Inn, the facsimile of the house of Shakespeare, the celebrated Butchart Gardens and (a first in North America) Butterflies World. Then, you might enjoy traveling by water from Vancouver Island to the beautiful city of Vancouver. There you will want to see the World's Fair facilities and so many other places, that you will need several days. The Museum of Anthropology there contains the largest collection of Indian carvings in the world. You can admire one of the finest collection of authentic totem poles along a portion of Canada Highway 16 (Yellowhead Highway) near the small town of Hazelton. And take the observatory train for an unforgettable trip in the awesome Rockies. Banff and Jasper national parks are wonderful places to camp.

I have been told that the West Edmonton Mall, the largest in the world, is worth the trip. It has an amusement park, enormous water slide, a skating rink and, yes, you can even go shopping. Visit Fort Edmonton Park (an outdoor museum) and the Space Sciences Center, the nation's largest planetarium. Try to be there for the gala Klondike Days during the last ten days of July, or plan to be in Calgary for the Calgary Stampede, each year in July. And, do not miss a chance to experience prehistory firsthand! Going east on highway 9 to Brumheller is the Tyrrell Museum of Paleontology, with the largest dinosaur display in the world, 200 of them.

Prince Albert National Park in Saskatchewan combines natural beauty with recreation. There you will find north country flora and fauna, which you can enjoy from a paddleboat trip. The southern part of the province harbors the wild, the ancient and the eccentric. In Manitoba, Winnipeg's fur trading past is honored at the Manitoba Museum of Man and Nature; its Ukrainian heritage, at the Ukrainian Cultural Center. Assiniboine Park contains a first rate zoo.

In Ontario the Talbot Trail skirts the northern shore of Lake Erie. One site along the way in Dresden is Uncle Tom's Cabin Museum. Toronto is a city that has almost everything, even old-fashioned tramways. You'll want to spend a few days there, for sure. To the northeast is Peterborough, location of the world's largest hydraulic lift lock.

Down on highway 401 is Loyalist country. Upper Canada Village, near Morrisburg, depicts life of those Americans who remained loyal to Britain and fled the U.S. during the Revolution. It is also the gateway to the Thousand Islands from which you can book a day cruise. Highway 16 north goes to Ottawa, Canada's capital, a neat and pretty city with many parks. You will want to visit the cathedral-like Parliament building (I fell in love with its round library). The ceremony of the changing of the guard takes place in the morning; it is just like the one in London. You will love the architecture of the Museum of the Civilization, and you will want to browse in the National Gallery. There is much to see at the National Museum of Science and Technology. It is also interesting to see the embassies of the different countries. There is a leisurely boat ride available to tourists on which a guide provides considerable information about the city.

Further east, you can enter the province of Quebec, where the majority of people do not speak English except at tourist places, big hotels and restaurants. So, do not be offended if someone does not answer you and does not seem friendly; he is probably embarrassed because he does not understand. So, just talk to someone else; many people do speak English, especialy around Montreal, a pretty and lively city built on an island around Mount-Royal. Like Toronto, it has almost everything, except with a French accent. Tourists have the impression they are in France. If you park your RV at the KOA Montreal South, you can join tours of the city right at the campground.

If you want some quiet quaintness, you'll find plenty of it in the Rivière-Du-Loup, where you can go around the Gaspé peninsula for some outstanding scenery. Or you may wish to travel to New Brunswick and the other maritime provinces, where there is a lot to see and communication is in English.

If you wish to tour the U.S.A., a great way to travel is to follow a special interest. For instance, someone who is greatly impressed by caverns might have compiled statistics and information about several he has heard or read about. The next step is to visit and compare them. This particular interest could take a person all over the country. The Southeast boasts the greatest number, but most states have caves, caverns or lava tubes. A wealth of these hidden worlds can be found in the national parks and state parks systems and other public lands, as well as in privately owned and operated properties. For newcomers to the activity, guided tours provide an introduction to the appreciation of caves, as well as information on the formation process.

The country's premier cave site is New Mexico's Carlsbad Caverns. Other huge ones are La Jolla Cave in southern California and the Sea Lion Caves in Oregon. There is the Russell Cave National Monument in Alabama, Mitchell Caverns in California, the Wind and Jewell caves in South Dakota, Mammoth Cave National Park in Kentucky and about 60 more in the U.S. alone. The simple perusal of an atlas will tell you where they are, but you may also want to look at the National Caves Directory.

Some RVers follow regattas; others visit baseball winter camps or follow tennis tournaments. If you are interested in any sport or hobby, follow it around the country, and see the beautiful U.S.A. (Please see Chapter 10 for additional suggestions.)

The First Winter of *New* Northern Nomads

In general, nomads follow the birds and go south in the fall and return north in the spring. The ones from the Northeast come down the coast, swim in the not yet too cold sea and loll on the deserted beaches. They may tour Florida and then head for California, with a detour to Mexico. In that way, the entire winter is spent in a warm climate. In the spring, they go up the Pacific coast, stop at Victoria (in what is jokingly called "tropical Canada") then start across Canada back to the East, with a head full of images and memories, to face the reality of income tax time. Many Northwesterners make the same journey, the other way around.

My husband and I made the trip. Before leaving, I believed that I only had to see a place once. I soon understood that it does not work that way. At least not for me. When I like a song I want to hear it again; it's the same for some places. Certain landscapes, certain cities impress or intrigue me and I plan to see them again. My traveling is far from over yet. There is a lot I have missed in North America, plus I want to see the rest of the world! I'll never have enough time to do it all!

CHAPTER 5

Why Join Camping Clubs?

Advantages and Services

If you want to make friends who share your interest in the world of RVing, join a club, and you will have people with whom you can exchange information. They will tell you about the best campgrounds, regions and cultures they especially enjoy, things "not to miss" all over America, and how to make your RV run smoothly and be more comfortable. Notwithstanding the great companionship, clubs offer many services. (No need to be a fulltimer to join any of these clubs) My favorite clubs include the Good Sam Club. The largest in the world with 800,000 member families, it is divided into fifty-six sections that include most states and many Canadian provinces. Each section is divided into regions and the regions into chapters. In Florida, for instance, there are eleven regions, each with chapters.

Each section has a director and assistants who organize rallies. In each state a big one, called Samboree, is slated each year and draws as many as 1,000 RVs. Participants join in games, tournaments, community meals, dances, shows, bingo, etc. RV salesmen are always present with their latest models and accessories, as well as people who make insignias, craftsmen who sell their work, etc.

For $15 a year, members receive transfers to display on their RVs or cars; 10% discount on gas bought with a Good Sam Visa card; 10% discount in the 2,000 campgrounds cataloged in the *Trailer Life Campground Directory*, also available for a discount; and 10% on parts and accessories purchased from participating dealers listed in this directory, along with the restaurants, theme parks and other attractions that give discounts. For a fee, members can subscribe to an emergency towing service. They also can use the Standby Sam list of members who have volunteered to help members in need in their area.

You can join an insurance group for medical and hospital care as well as life insurance. You receive a 50% discount on *Trailer Life* and *Motorhome* magazines, and 10% on propane you buy at CalGas. You can open a Sam Cash money market account at reasonable interest and have access to this money at 17,500 automatic tellers worldwide. You are offered a route tracing service, a mail forwarding service, free registration of credit cards in case of theft or loss, a lost key service, a lost pet service, a travel agency, vehicle insurance, RV financing, plus a free subscription to the monthly *Hi-Way Herald*.

The Family Motor Coach Association (FMCA) is the biggest club for motorhomes and self-contained camping vans, and has more than 100,000 member families. It is divided into over 200 chapters (I belong to two: Singles International and Fulltimers). This club offers free accident insurance, free mail forwarding and phone message services, motorhome financing, a theft-protection sticker offering a $200 reward for info concerning the theft of your RV, and a free KOA card, which gives a 10% discount in 500 campgrounds. FMCA offers an excellent road emergency service, which I use, also a 10% discount to the Outdoor Resort Campgrounds of America, a 10% discount on rental cars, a six-month discount at Camping World for repairs and accessories; and a driver for your RV if you must fly home. Each month you receive a superb magazine with loads of information for the RVer; in the January issue, there is a list of the chapters, all the members and those who invite others to stop for a chat, overnight camping or for mechanical help. The chapters plan many rallies, but the ones you should not miss are the extraordinary conventions the FMCA head office organizes twice a year. This is where I was able to examine those $700,000 super bus/motorhomes and the amazing Cloud Liner.

At one of the conventions in Tampa, Florida, the Full-timers chapter was responsible for the pre-convention parking on a lot near the site of the convention. As a member of this chapter, I volunteered and this is where, with the help of Joe Milan, president of the chapter, I learned a new skill— parking attendant. This retired colonel quickly made me understand that when I signalled drivers to clear the road it must not look like a salute because those who knew me had a tendency to stop and talk with me, thereby blocking the road. When all the motorhomes had been parked (sometimes these big, expensive buses came four or five in a file, towing small cars such as Porsches, Mercedes, Jaguars), Joe and Agnes invited me to have a drink under their awning with other volunteers who were sharing the funny experiences of the day.

Even as a widow, I do not feel left out with the RVers. As a matter of fact, if I really want to enjoy myself and meet amusing people, I found out I need to volunteer to help at a rally.

A lot goes on at a FMCA Convention. In the summer of '87 at DesMoines, the capital of Iowa, there was an organized tour of the city, of course, which included free coffee and doughnuts served by the Bluebird (bus/motorhomes) Company, to the sound of a jazz orchestra (at 8:00 A.M. we were awake fast!). There were aerobic classes, square dancing, a magician, a juggler, a quartet, some acrobats, a clown, a ventriloquist, music by the Frustrated Maestros, tap dancers, an accordian player, a caricaturist, a balloon distributor, ice cream treats, a horse shoe tournament, a fashion show and movies. All these were presented at different booths around the grounds.

During the evenings, acrobats from China, magicians, a steel band and the famous Phyllis Diller performed and we were invited to dance to the sounds of a big band. During those three days, several chapters held their meetings. Then, there were the seminars: maintenance, basic mechanics and preventive driving for ladies only, mechanics for men, full-time nomad life given by the Fulltimers, interior decoration of RVs, cooking with microwaves, insurance, RVs in Mexico, the magic of jewels and doll making, and of course, the RV show with the accent on the biggest and the best. Plus, there were additional activities within each chapter since their members were parked together.

At the Tampa Convention, I was very busy. My mini-motorhome was parked with the Singles International to which I belong; however, I sometimes left the cocktail parties of this chapter to join the Fulltimers' party. What a life for $25 a year to be an FMCA member and display the black oval logo ($35 the first year).

Another group is the Escapees (SKPs), a club founded for fulltime nomads and those considering becoming one. The aim of its founders was to help the 16,000 member families to Share Knowledge and Pleasure. Like other RV clubs, Escapees has chapters that host rallies across America.

For $40 ($45 the first year) any camper can join the club and get a membership card, logo to display, the membership directory, and the list of SKPers who offer free parking at their homes. Membership includes free parking at SKP retreats and co-ops and a bimonthly newsletter packed with information on ways to cut RVing expenses and enrich your travels. There are technical articles on maintenance and customizing RVs for maximum self-sufficiency, articles on subsidizing income and house-keeping tips. A section lists free parking spots found by the members; another section allows you to keep track of the friends you have met in your travels.

Members get discounts at certain campgrounds, as well as low rental serviced sites at SKP retreats and co-op parks. They can also buy a lot in private co-ops, mostly in southern U.S.A., for from $2,500 to $9,000. For a fee, a member can use the mail message service, join other chapters, and attend rallies. Especially recommended are the two annual Escapades, where you can learn more in a week than in years of trial and error.

When you meet an SKP, even if you do not know him or her, you give a hug. It's a congenial form of instant camaraderie. We engage in The Hug Therapy (from *Better Times*)

Doesn't a hug always make you feel better? There's a reason. Aside from the fact it's usually nice to be touched, scientists have found physical contact to be essential to our emotional well-being. Of all the forms of touching, hugging is the most therapeutic. A hug can dispel loneliness, ease tension and help you fall asleep. Plus, you can do it anywhere! What could be better?

There are many other camping clubs you can join; I will only name a few more: Friendly Roamers, the National Campers and Hikers Association, S.M.A.R.T., and Military Living for active or retired members. Certain brand names of RVs have their own clubs, such as Airstream, Coachmen, Winnebago, etc. When you buy an RV, even a second-hand one, ask the manufacturer. (See Chapter 1 for information about clubs and chapters for singles only.) With all the decals on your RV, the chance is good that interested persons will come to talk to you, to ask for information or to discuss the last rally they attended or the unusual places that they have just visited.

A few days before Thanksgiving one fall, I was coming back from a meeting of the Florida Sunseekers SKP chapter, when, thanks to a LOW sticker, which attracted my attention, I recognized Ruth Lawson in a micro-mini that I passed. She is the secretary of a LOW chapter. We agreed to stop at the next MacDonald's. After a big hug, we talked about the meeting of the LOW rally that I missed and about the meeting of the Florida Sunseekers that she missed, and brought our personal news up to date. Then she invited me to celebrate Thanksgiving with her in Orlando, with other members of LOW and two SKPs that I knew from a rally in Montreal. Our individual RVs parked on her large property would permit us to celebrate until late and leave the next morning.

Codes of Ethics

Most camping clubs have a code of ethics. The purpose is to promote safety and create a desirable public image of RVers as responsible drivers and good citizens. Remember that the public judges all campers by the action of individual campers, and adhere to a few basic rules:

- Carry appropriate insurance on your vehicle to protect others in case of an accident.
- Obey all federal, state, provincial and local laws regarding the ownership and driving of a vehicle.
- Respect the rights and privacy of other campers on and off the highways.
- Offer to aid other campers in difficulty.
- Make sure your guests obey the rules.

Concerning your vehicle, you should:

- Maintain it in good mechanical condition so it does not become a menace on the highways.
- Be certain all exterior lights, including hazard lights, are operable and use directional signals consistently when making a turn.
- Use adequate rear-view mirrors.
- Keep your adequate size tires in good condition and properly inflated according to gross weight.
- Carry a working fire extinguisher of the proper type.
- Carry currently dated flares or operable emergency signal devices.
- Use wheel-blocking devices to keep your vehicle safely immobile when necessary.
- Locate all batteries in a ventilated compartment and maintain them on schedule.
- Carry LP gas containers upright in a ventilated compartment.
- Use the new and safe equipment if you tow a trailer or other vehicle, and have it inspected regularly. Check frequently to make certain that running lights and turn signal connections are sound.

When you are on the road:

- Never operate a vehicle in an unsafe manner or in unsafe mechanical condition except to get to the nearest point of repair.
- Never drive when you do not feel well or when you are emotionally unstable.
- Never be a road block or traffic hazard for others. On a narrow road, pull off to let others pass if a line of cars is behind you.
- When you are traveling with others, leave enough distance

between vehicles to allow other drivers to safely pass each unit.

- Tie down securely all objects being carried outside the vehicle.
- Completely close holding tanks to ensure against leaks.
- Never discard anything anywhere but in the proper trash containers or ashtrays.

When you are parked:

- Do not remain overnight in a shopping center or on other private property without asking permission. If possible, affix proof of permission on a vehicle window.
- Comply with all rules of the parks.
- Park only where you do not interfere with others.
- Avoid making excessive noise late at night or early in the morning.
- Try to have an observer help with the blind spots when parking or backing up.
- Avoid damaging trees, shubbery, flowers, etc.
- Keep pets on a leash unless permission is obtained for their release. Remove their excrement.
- Do not dispose of liquid waste on the ground.
- Extinguish completely all campfires, matches, cigarettes.
- Wear acceptable clothing and use decent language. In other words, preserve the reputation of all campers.

CHAPTER 6

How Do You Get Money on the Road?

Due to constant improvements in technology, banking services change very rapidly. For updated information, ask your bank manager what will work best for you.

To be sure to have enough money in the bank while you are traveling, make arrangements to have all your regular income checks deposited directly into your account. That way, you don't have to rely on anyone else to deposit your money or worry about the mail being late, the checks being stolen, etc.

Personal Checks

As a rule, you cannot rely on personal checks to pay for anything while on the road. The exception might be if you happen to be in a state where you have a bank account. If you go to a bank to cash a personal check, unless you have the collateral right there, it will take up to ten days before it clears and you can get the cash. Even with a certified or a cashier's check, you could have trouble in some banks because of the prevalence of forgery. And, of course, be prepared to show identity such as a passport, driver's license, Social Security card, and preferably an official card with your photo. When you run into a problem, offer to pay for a call to your bank or ask to see the manager; he or she might choose to bend the rules.

If you plan to stay in a town for a while, you might want to open an account with a check from home. Every bank has all kinds of accounts, some with freebies for people 55 and over. It's recommended that you start numbering checks with number 100, so it does not appear that you have a brand new account; you will be trusted more. It is advisable to remember to deal with a bank using the same ATM (Automated Teller Machine) system or systems used by your home bank in order to get easy access to your funds wherever you happen to be. And, keep trying to pay everything with checks; it works sometimes and saves trips to the bank.

Travelers' Checks

When we started our nomad life, my husband and I were using travelers' checks. We found them useful for our occasional trips in the Caribbean, the United States, Europe and Canada. But for yearlong use they were too inconvenient. You pay a percentage at the time of purchase plus you lose the interest this money would have earned if you had left it in the bank. You also have to keep a record of checks you have used in case you lose any and want to make a claim. If you travel with someone else, you both must have some checks in each name so you will have money when you are separated, which complicates the record keeping. If you need more checks while traveling, you can purchase them at banks, but there are problems involved in transferring funds. There are agents at airports and major hotels where you can buy them with a bank card identification, but you seldom are in these places when you are a nomad.

We wasted a lot of time once when we tried to purchase checks in San Diego. We found the address in the information that came with our card. It took us nearly an hour to find the office, in a small shopping center in a residential section of the city, where there was a sign in the window telling us they had moved. We found the new location on our city map—it was at the other side of town. We spent another hour getting there. We gave them a check for $1,000 from our Canadian bank, of course, with "U.S. funds" beside the amount. After checking the validity of our card, they called our bank and were supposed to give us $800 in travelers' checks and $200 in cash, but they didn't have enough cash. We had to accept the $200 in checks, and, of course, pay the fee on them too.

Sometimes it's rather complicated to use these checks. In Miami, a store cashier sent me to the manager. I've heard that some stores have refused the checks! So, I really don't think they're practical for year round traveling.

Credit Cards

The most practical way to pay for purchases is with the cards that banks and other financial institutions give you to use in the automated teller machines (ATMs). Get them now and/or raise your credit limit to the maximum. You can use them almost anywhere, but you still need cash. Some gas stations don't accept them or charge more when you pay with them. I don't think you need gasoline or other cards unless you get extra benefits when you use them (inquire). Visa, Mastercard and American Express are accepted almost everywhere, even in some grocery stores (like Albertson's in Florida), Seven Elevens, liquor stores, garages, RV dealers, doctors, lawyers, even hospitals. It does not cost more to have a high credit limit, and, should you have to use it, you don't pay interest if you pay back within the time limit.

When you get the bills from your credit cards, you mail a check drawn on your home bank account. You have to be sure you get your bill on time; in case you don't, send a check ahead of time in order not to pay interest.

Debit Cards

Visa and other debit cards are a more recent development. To use them, you first have to have a deposit in a bank or other financial institution. When you use a debit card to pay for something, the amount is automatically deducted from your total deposit, so you don't have to later send a check.

Needed Cash

When you need money away from home, it's not easy to get cash with a personal check. The easiest and most practical way to obtain needed cash is with credit and debit cards. You make arrangements with your home bank for a card and a secret code. Then you can use your card in an ATM and get a few hundred dollars everyday just about anywhere in the world, as long as there is money in your bank account.

When you need more money than is left in your account, you can walk into a bank and ask for a cash advance. They will give you the money right away, after getting approval from your card headquarters. However, since this is a loan you start paying interest immediately that will show on your next statement.

There are other ways to obtain cash, which are usually slower and more complicated. One is the American Express MoneyGram system. It is rather involved, so inquire about it from American Express. Citicorp has a similar system; your bank should be able to give you information. Western Union offices have been sending money for ages; check with one of their offices listed in the phone book.

Paying Bills

Like everyone else, I receive bills for insurance, telephone calls, credit cards, club membership fees. All I have to do is mail a check from my home bank. If I have paid for purchases in a foreign country with my credit card, the statement will show the amount of the purchase in my country's funds according to the exchange rate on the day of the purchase.

There are other ways to pay. Some bills can be paid through a bank. You either go yourself to the bank, use an ATM, pay by phone (a touchtone one) or, you may make prior arrangements to have your regular bills sent to the bank, and the amount debited from your account. Inquire at your bank or other financial institution and find out what is best for you. Some of these services cost a few dollars, but if it gives you peace of mind and makes your life easier, I personally think it's worth it.

CHAPTER 7

How Do You Deal with Emergencies?

Medical Problems

The fear of becoming sick or hurt thousands of miles from one's own doctor keeps many mature people from traveling. Often people say things like: "I would like to travel, but my wife has had a heart attack," or "I cannot go too far; I never know when I might need to go back to the hospital."

It's normal that with the passing years, we develop some health problems; and it is also normal to feel more secure staying close to a familiar doctor. However, when we cannot change some of life's misfortunes, we surely can change our attitude in the face of them.

Who's to say that when I need my doctor, he will not be off on a trip? Even if I go only to San Diego and I get sick there, my Los Angeles doctor will be of no help . . . and there are good ones in San Diego too. More and more people travel; a majority of them are retirees who were never free to travel before. Do you believe they are all in perfectly good health?

Newell Knapp, a 90-year-old man, traveled fulltime in his Airstream trailer; he used to say, "You can use all kinds of excuses to stay home, too bad for you!"

Unless you're traveling in a jungle, you'll receive medical attention if you need it. Do not worry; all doctors have an obligation to do their best for any patient, whether they know him or not.

I can speak from experience since I have become sick a few times during my travels. I have been taken care of as well as when I was sick in my hometown. Once I was rushed to a Miami hospital for, what we thought to be, a heart attack. Nobody knew me there; yet, I doubt I would have been met and taken care of more diligently if I had been a celebrity.

Prevention

There are some precautions you should take to minimize the risks of an emergency and to facilitate the task of those who might have to help you should an emergency arise.

It is important to get sufficient exercise and eat sensibly to prevent deterioration. Protect yourself from sunburns and use good sense when participating in sports and on the water. Have regular check-ups and work at correcting problems. Ask your doctor for a written report on your condition if you have a health problem. He should list your medications, why, when and how you take them and possible side effects or interactions.

Ask your doctor to prescribe enough pills, syringes, etc., for the duration of time you'll be away; it will save difficulties, particularly in a foreign country where drugs may be sold under other names. He should tell you about vaccines and any precautions to take. He could help you prepare a first aid box. If your blood pressure is a problem, a nurse can show you how to take it yourself.

Whether you travel or not, you should be ready for an

emergency to happen when you are alone. If you have a health problem, wear a Medic-Alert bracelet. A "Vial of Life" with your medical history should be kept in your fridge with a sticker on the fridge door and RV entrance door. Another "Vial of Life" should be kept in the glove compartment of your tow car and a sticker on the windshield plus the card in your wallet. It will inform those caring for you that you are allergic to something, or that you are deaf, have diabetes or a heart problem. It could save your life should you lose consciousness, with no one near who knows your problems.

A nurse, who worked for eight years in an emergency room of a hospital, said she often met people who were not at all prepared for this eventuality. It is not enough to tell emergency personnel you suffer from heart disease for which you have to take a small pink pill. Too many patients rely totally on their doctor: "Phone my doctor; I can call him anytime." What an illusion! Try to call a doctor in the middle of the night. . . . And if you do reach him, chances are he will not remember you at all and will not have access to your records. Some people assume their spouses will be able to provide the necessary information, but very often the partner is not present or is too upset. So, here is a suggestion from the nurse: everyone should carry information about his own and his partner's physical condition and medications on a card in his wallet. And don't forget to up-date it! But, keep in mind that paramedics don't have time to search for vital information, and if you're in an accident a wallet might be lost. If you have special health needs get a bracelet and the "Vial of Life"! In addition, everyone should take a Red Cross first aid course and know how to do CPR.

Even if you don't intend now to travel in another country, you might decide quite abruptly to do so. If you're RVing in northern U.S.A., you might want to go across the border into Canada. It is best to determine ahead of time that your medical coverage, as well as auto insurance, is valid outside the country. Another kind of insurance that can save you from frustrating situations is that provided by carrying spare contact lenses, glasses and dentures with you.

Dealing with Medical Emergencies

Despite all precaution, everyone gets sick, sooner or later. When it's not an emergency, some RVers consult the A.M.A. Medical Guide, the book *Merck* for diseases and the book *Drugs* for over-the-counter drugs; they are all on sale at bookstores. Some try a long distance call to a personal physician for suggestions of over-the-counter drugs or a prescription. Walgreen's drugstores have a computer system that provides nationwide access to pharmaceutical records of every Walgreen.

When you need a doctor, ask the campground management for the address of a walk-in clinic nearby or for directions to the nearest hospital. Look for the "H" signs, and often you'll find a clinic right next to many hospitals. If you are referred to a specialist for an appointment several days later, explain that you're just passing through and offer to pay bills with a credit card. Doctors are wary of non-residents who collect insurance money and never reimburse them. You can always ask for reimbursement later from your insurance.

A pharmacist can also probably give you the name of a doctor who will take new patients. If you have to consult a doctor with an established practice, don't make an appointment; it's too easy to refuse someone on the phone. Instead, walk in, explain your situation and be sure to mention payment by cash or credit card.

If you are very sick and need immediate care, don't be foolish and drive yourself. Call 911, the operator, or the police and ask for an ambulance. You will have help in minutes and treatment right there, in radio contact with hospital specialists. (This is good advice, whether you leave home or not.)

To be ready for an emergency right on the road, carry a sign with "Call the Police" on one side and "Call 911 for Doctor" on the other. If you're sick, park your vehicle securely on the side of the road, dial 9 on your CB and ask for an ambulance, and put your sign in the windshield. Wherever, you're parked, you can blow your horn and flash your lights; someone will come and see what's going on.

Contrary to what you may think, there are advantages to being sick while RVing. The first time I was hospitalized, in Miami, my husband parked our motorhome in the hospital parking lot. (Some hospitals have their own RV parking, like Columbus Hospital of Great Falls, Montana). It was easy for him to visit me, and if I needed something, he went down to get it from "our house." At the end of my stay, I came out of the hospital in my pajamas, entered my home right in front of the door, changed into my bathing suit and went directly and happily to the beach.

Another winter, in another hospital, when I awoke after an operation, my husband, reassured, went down to our RV. He preferred to rest in the comfort of "his home" instead of sitting by the side of a drugged lady. The personnel of the hospital knew he was right there in the parking lot, and they could have fetched him if necessary.

The convalescence period in an RV is easy. Perfect. Lying down on my bed, I could see the skies and the trees; I could hear the birds singing. I just had to stretch my arm to open the window or to pull the curtains. Housekeeping was much easier for my husband than if we had been in a regular house. It was less boring for him in a campground. He could play shuffleboard (he loved the game) and join card games or play pool while I was sleeping or reading; he was never far away. I only had a few steps to get to the door and two steps down to be outside, where I could recline in my lounge chair. Other campers had heard about my stay in the hospital and came to inquire about my experience.

They felt sorry for me that I was away from my father, sisters, kids and old friends. When something happens, you like to have your family with you, but, on the other hand, they would have worried for nothing. I had asked Lucien, my husband, not to phone them until the operation was over. There was nothing they could do. After everything was OK, I started getting calls and flowers and all was fine. I was happy to hear familiar voices on the phone.

Mechanical Difficulties

Almost every time someone interviews me on the radio or on RV, I am asked what I do, a woman alone, if I have a flat tire. Well, so far, I've never had one. But since I never changed a tire when I was driving a car, I sure will not try to do it on a 11,000-pound vehicle! The same applies for any mechanical problem I have; I call a garage. Once my RV just stopped right on the road. I dialled 9 on my CB and told the police I needed a mechanic for a sick, heavy RV. They sent one, and after checking under the hood, he towed my "home" to a garage where I learned the bad news: my RV needed a new heart. As a FMCA member, I was a member of the Road Vantage Towing Road Service, so I called their toll-free number and reported my predicament. All I had to do was to sign the towing bill; they paid it. As for the motor, I had to wait three days to get a new one and to have it installed. Since I was at a large GM dealer garage with strict insurance restrictions, I could not stay in my RV overnight. But they drove me to a nice motel where I had no choice but to work on my first book (no more distractions with friends and rallies) while basking in the sun or enjoying the pool.

Of course, when something like this happens, I first get very annoyed. Who wouldn't? But I calm down eventually after reminding myself that the same thing could happen with a car.

Prevention of Mechanical Problems

In the episode above, there was no lack of preventive maintenance involved; it was a defective rod that broke, a very rare occurrence. An RV and/or towing vehicle should be periodically checked and maintained just as a car. You should carry extra motor oil and other fluids, spare belts and a spare wheel. (Some RVs are sold without one and the proper size tire is frequently hard to find.) It's also a good idea to carry booster cables.

Taking Action in a Mechanical Emergency

In an emergency, it is often better to be in an RV than in an ordinary car. For instance, if you stall in the middle of the road, you are safer in a motorhome than in a mini-compact car. (But, you can push a little car to the side of the road.) With an RV, you are more likely to have a radio to call for help. There is a high probability that someone will trust an RV owner enough to stop and help. Most other RVers will, anyway. On the other hand, the majority of drivers will not stop for a car.

In an emergency, get off the road; if it's impossible, don't stay in the car or the RV. Put a white piece of cloth on the driver's side mirror, or place cardboard signs with "Help" on the windshield and the back window. Put the emergency brakes on and the transmission in park. Set phosphorescent triangles or other signalling devices behind the vehicle to warn oncoming motorists. You can even use rocks like they do in Mexico. If you are on a slope, turn and block the wheels or put boards under the frame or the bumper.

If your vehicle is not parked in a vulnerable position, but you are wary of the area, be prudent and stay in your car or

RV. When someone comes to help, hand him a quarter without lowering your window very far, and ask him to call for help. If there is no emergency, you can always call an RV club member who lives in the area. FMCA and Good Sam provide a list of the members who are ready to help.

You could also refer to the *RV Repair & Maintenance Manual* or *Chevrolet Motorhome Chassis Service Guide* or check your *Recreational Vehicle Service Directory* or your *U-Haul RV Centers Directory*.

Hopefully taking precautions and being prepared will keep you from ever having to deal with an emergency situation.

CHAPTER 8

How Does Your Family Keep in Contact with You?

Mail

I have often been asked, "What are the inconveniences of this lifestyle?" Everytime, I am at a loss. Probably, I don't think of them anymore because I'm so well accustomed to them. There is one, however, that comes to mind. You can't travel according to your whims and get your mail at the door each morning, but there are many ways to minimize the problem.

A friend of mine has all his mail delivered to his daughter. She opens his mail, manages his investments, takes care of his deposits. She has a joint account with him and pays his bills, buys family gifts for him, pays for his phone calls, etc. He calls her regularly; she gives him the news and he gives her his instructions. He has nothing to worry about; she takes care of everything.

This is a acceptable way of managing for many nomads and it's a fact that mail may be less important for some persons than it is for others. Personally, even if I don't love keeping my checkbook up to date and paying bills, I love to get letters from my family and my friends and I want to know what's going on with the new friends I have made and with the RV clubs I belong to.

The best way to be 99% sure of receiving all your mail is to use a mail forwarding service. If you prefer the services of a friend or a family member, there are a few points to consider. First, choose someone who likes to write letters, so he understands how important the mail is to you. This person should be reliable, orderly, punctual, healthy and able to go to the post office, someone who is stable and will not move. It must be someone who will not tire of the responsibility after a few months. It may become too much of a chore for many people, and "that wonderful person might become negligent and unreliable—what can you say if it's being done as a favor? Many nomads have been in this situation before they started using a mail forwarding service.

I use the FMCA club service. It's free for club members. All I have to pay is the postage; I am not even charged for the envelopes. I give the service's address to everyone, except to the government, to insurance companies and others who need to know my official residence. To be sure not to miss anyone I file a "change-of-address" card with my post office showing my mail forwarding service as my new address.

All my mail goes to the service—eventually. I call them at a toll-free number and tell them where and until what date I want to receive my mail. Once a week, everything is put in a large brown envelope, on which is printed: "Wait for Arrival." If there is much mail and they use two envelopes, they print on the first "One of Two" and on the second "Two of Two."

When I retrieve my mail I make sure the postal or campground clerk looks into the special box for incoming large envelopes. When you give instructions to the service, you tell them if they are valid for only this once or for many weeks. If for only one week and they have no additional instructions, they simply hold my mail until I notify them again. I can spend as much time on the road following my whims as I wish.

The service is located in Ohio and sends out my mail every Thursday. Allowing for holidays and unexpected delays, I can figure out fairly accurately where I want it delivered. If I choose to be "delayed" en route, I make sure to give the service an address where my mail can wait, like the General Delivery of the post office of a small town where I am sure to go. I don't use big city post offices; you never know where to pick up your mail.

You might plan to have your mail delivered to a campground; most managers are careful with mail. If you're not sure, use the General Delivery of the nearest post office. If you leave before receiving mail you know was addressed to a campground, make sure you leave instructions with the manager; a post office will not forward mail addressed to a campground. One of the many advantages of my mail service is that I get my mail once a week, all together, in a large envelope. I don't have to worry about it. Remember that only parcels delivered by U.S. mail will be accepted at General Delivery. A UPS delivery must go to a street address.

Telephone

A few years ago, when the cellular phones became readily available, everybody told me I should have one. My inquiries showed they were expensive to buy and to operate and their use was limited to a few large metropolitan areas. Now, I read they are much improved and I might, just might, get one; what makes me uncertain is that I have a "free" set-up that works and I am used to it. So, for now, I can only advise you to check out the cellular system after reading about my system which is also the one thousands of other RVers are using. Some RVers use a pager. It might be worthwhile to inquire.

I was working as a realtor when I retired; so you can understand how important the telephone was for me at the time. I could not go into the garden without having a phone by my side. At one time, I used a pager in my handbag, a mobile phone in my car and an answering machine with remote access on my home phone. With an office that was taking my messages plus an answering service for non-business hours, I was always accessible. In my imagination, I saw myself dangling at the end of a telephone line, holding the receiver with all my might. Now? Nothing but peace and quiet. I have learned to appreciate not being disturbed while I am looking at a good TV movie. Would I want a cellular phone?

At the beginning of this nomad life, everyone is worried. Letters are not enough. We mail cassettes back and forth, but what we really want is to communicate by telephone. You can write and tell your son to call you at a certain time, on a certain day. It is embarrassing for you because your son will pay and will not want to be reimbursed. And that "appointment" is annoying for everyone concerned, especially for you, who have to be there and waiting. When you are a nomad, you don't like commitments any more. For more freedom, you can write that you will phone him on a certain day, at a specific time (from wherever you will be).

You get yourself plenty of change and phone from a telephone booth. Or you can make the call collect and then the person called will never want to send you the bill (embarrassing again). Or, you can save money by direct calling (no operator intervention) from a friend's, but he might never want to send you the bill when he gets it. Or you can time the call (if you ask the operator to do it, it will not be a direct call) and price the call yourself, using the rates in the phone book; but your friend might refuse the money you offer. You

A FEW RECREATIONAL VEHICLES

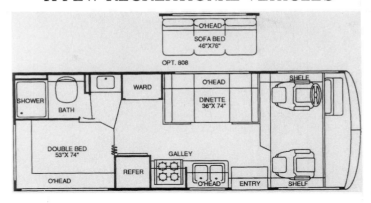

Courtesy of FLEETWOOD ENTERPRISES, INC.

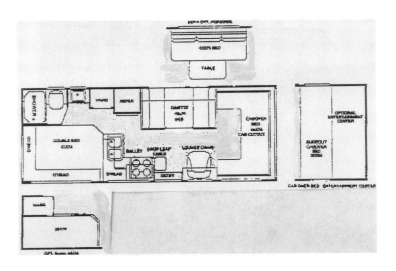

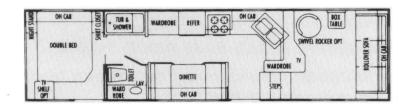

NIGHT STAND · OH CAB · SHIRT CLOSET · TUB & SHOWER · WARDROBE · REFER · OH CAB · BOX TABLE · SWIVEL ROCKER OPT · ROLLOVER SOFA · OH CAB · DOUBLE BED · TV · WARDROBE · TV SHELF OPT · TOILET · LAV · WARD ROBE · DINETTE · OH CAB · STEPS

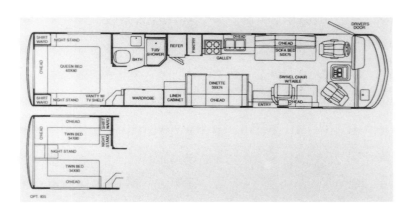

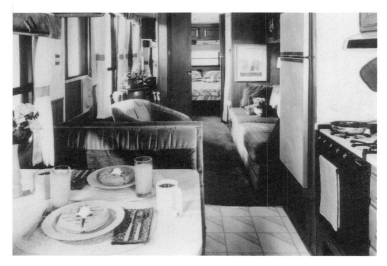

can also ask the operator to bill your son's number (a third party) and you'll pay him later.

There are disadvantages to all of the above ways, obviously. The best way to place a call is to use a calling card. If you have no phone of your own, ask for one with a ficticious number. (You might have to speak to many people at the telephone company; not many know about these cards.) I use one and get my bills at my mail service with no extra charge for long distance calls; my Bell Canada card is free. It is probably the same with other companies, but whatever small fee they might charge, it's worth it for the convenience of having a card. There is no need for piles of coins. You just dial "O" before an area code and the number you want to reach and give the card number to the operator, or in many areas you just punch it.

My personal set-up is using the free telephone message service offered by FMCA to its members. I give the toll-free 800 number (the same one I use for my mail service) to everyone and if they phone between 8 a.m. and 11 p.m. Monday through Friday, they quote my club member number and leave a message. They can also ask for my general message, which tells them where I can be reached (if I wish). It is always up to me to call my service, using the same toll-free number, to get my messages. I then return my calls, using my calling card. So simple! Sometimes my callers are right in the same town I happen to call from . . . so, we meet right there! Like its mail forwarding service, this FMCA telephone messages service is fantastic. There are other clubs and companies that offer similar services which give peace of mind to me and to anyone concerned about me.

Another fantastic way to keep in touch with your family and the whole world is amateur radio! If you are an operator, you are very fortunate! There is an AM radio chapter with FMCA.

CHAPTER 9

How Do You Cope with the Separation from Your Family?

Bad and Good Points

It is an undeniable fact, for me and most nomads I know, that we do miss our friends and family. How many times have I wished I were rich enough to rent an RV or two and invite them all to come caravaning with me for a few weeks? This way, they could live with me and we could share the same experiences. Would that not be fantastic? Sometimes I dream of such a possibility while traveling along some beautiful country road. There must be some lucky RVers who can afford to do it; I don't happen to know any.

The worst part of the separation is parting company. To say, "Goodbye, see you in six months," is far from easy. For example, in the fall when I leave Canada, my son Pierre and his family, my father and his wife, my sisters and their families, it is difficult for me. During the summer, I have shared the lives of all these people so important to me; often I have taken part in their projects and their dreams. I would love to continue witnessing the development of my grand-children! And then, there are my very good friends with whom life and confidences are so easy.

I leave behind a part of my life sadly, but willingly; I realize that I cannot live others' lives nor even on the border of their lives. I am at a different stage of existence than my children are, and I have different interests. Since it is impossible to go right and left at the same time, I have to make a choice.

I must say, though, that I went on six-weeks-long trips to Europe and Florida for several consecutive years before my first six-month tour around the U.S.A., Mexico and Canada in a travel trailer with my husband. The following year we started our life year round in a thirty-foot motorhome. I and my family got used to this separation gradually.

Most fulltimers tell me they started by going South for two or three months at first. Then, they did not like the cold anymore, so they left for six months; then they found their house too big and too much trouble for only six months and started living year round in their RV.

There are always two sides to a story. When I come back in the spring, I am welcomed with open arms like a very impor-tant visitor, a kind of V.I.P. . . . I would not get such a reception if I were always around! I am told that I bring sunshine and a good sign that summer is around the corner, especially because of my suntan. The kids think it's Christ-mas all over again when I arrive with gifts for all of them. Recently I brought souvenirs from Mexico for everyone. I have also collected my impressions of this country for a magazine article; showing these writings make it easier to share my trip with my family. I have a coin collection from Mexico for my grandson Eric who spent a summer at his other grandmother's in France. He is collecting coins from different countries of Europe and from all his grandfather's friends. He now has a new interest that I started. My grand-kids like, of course, the T-shirts and other souvenirs I bring them from all over. But, what they enjoy most is when I invite them and their friends to have breakfast in my mini-motorhome and then take them to school. You should hear the explanations they give their friends when they show them around my little house! They also love to attend camping club rallies with their "funny grandma," as they call me sometimes.

Living in an RV is very practical. You can visit family and friends without preventing them from carrying on with their lives. You won't even dirty their sheets! I can enjoy a visit and be comfortable in my own bed with no need to pack a suitcase. I park in the driveway and my hosts come in for a drink and to see if I have made any changes in my "house." I take them out for dinner by the lake where I prepare the meal while we watch a regatta. Other times, we meet in front of a restaurant and I serve cocktails in my "home" before going into the restaurant for dinner.

When I visit my friends and family in the north in the summertime, we have so many things to say and do together, that six months go by much too fast. It starts getting cold and it's time to leave before I know it. And you know what? I never have time to talk about my sore legs and other aches and pains.

While I am gone, I keep in touch with friends and family with phone calls and letters. I send photos and I receive some that I post on the fridge just as I did in my former house. I send postcards, lots of them, so my family and my friends feel like they are traveling with me. If they want to contact me, they can do so through my service (see Chapter 8). Sometimes, family or friends come to see me. I make arrangements for their accommodations and rental cars or for a campsite. We have had some good times.

Holiday Times

For the majority of people, Christmas means family reunions and gift exchanges. Many grandparents enjoy celebrating holidays this way and they are lucky. But others have children who live in another province, another state and sometimes in another country. Due to studies or jobs, they cannot gather for celebrations at their parents' homes. Parents who are divorced and remarried may have three or four sets of grandparents to which they want to take the children on that day.

If you have a widely scattered family like I do, with a son in British Columbia, another in Quebec and a daughter in Florida, it's almost impossible to get them all together for any occasion, whether you are home or not. So . . . don't be sad about it. Make the best of the situation.

Some fulltime RVers can afford to pay for a trip south for their kids and grandkids. They arrange for them to stay in a hotel near the campground and they all have a ball. That's great, and if you have the money, better enjoy it together!

Many of you readers have family established just about everywhere and are waiting for them to be free to visit you. You may have to travel a long distance to visit just a few days, and may even then feel that you are in the way. Living in an RV, you can visit one household during the holidays and visit the others, one by one, throughout the rest of the year.

It is better this way. Grandchildren are never at ease too long in a grandparent's home. In an RV you can see them in their own homes with their friends. You can welcome them home from school and really see how they live, but you will always be out of their way in the comfort of your familiar home on wheels.

I have in the past spent Christmas without my children because it was impossible to be together. But there are so many other days in a year when my family and I were happy to be together, so many opportunities to say "I LOVE YOU" by letter or phone, that I would not let one day out of 365 depress me when things are not like in the movies.

At Christmas time, it is important to give some of ourselves to the ones we love. But it is also important to share with strangers, to make a small gesture that means "I care about you. . . . I am interested in you." After all, Christmas is in our hearts and can happen wherever we are. If you are a member of some of the clubs I've suggested, you can have a choice of Christmas celebrations to attend. All commercial campgrounds in the South also have Christmas parties. If you prefer to camp in a national forest, you can organize a small party with the neighbors; they'll love you for it. When you happen to meet them during your future travels, you can reminisce about it and they will thank you. You could plan to spend Christmas with your church. To find the nearest one wherever you travel send for the Directory of Churches in the USA.

Presently, it is my good fortune that I am able to spend December 25 with my daughter and her family. But, like other wanderers, I celebrate Christmas more than once. I will be with my son and his family in Montreal on October 25th. This is my Canadian Xmas.

Keeping Up with Friends

Psychologists recommend that people over fifty-five make a conscious effort to increase their circle of friends in order to replace those who have departed. Doing this promotes a healthy mental attitude and a sense of physical well being. Fulltime nomads are constantly meeting new people and accepting them as friends. They know that "a stranger is a friend not yet discovered" and rare are the cases when they do not, at least, learn something from these strangers. Often a friendship develops that will be maintained by phone calls, letters and meetings, planned and impromptu.

One day a woman named Colleen said to me, "I talk to a lot of fulltime nomads. Sometimes, we become very good friends in three days and we exchange confidences such as I never would have done with my longtime friends when I was living in my hometown. These new friends are all like me, happy, living as a nomad. At the moment, at least, I prefer making friends while traveling to living alone in an apartment, watching TV and attending senior citizens meetings where one always sees the same people."

Then there is Macbeth. Twice we happened to be at the same campground. At each place, she was spending two months, and everybody who knew her loved her. Maybe it was because she liked everybody. She had been a fulltime nomad since 1976 and said she was never bored. When it was raining, she sewed for a neighbor or made gifts for one of her grandchildren. She swims everyday and teaches knitting; she says it keeps her arthritis under control. During the summer, I hear that she does volunteer work at an hospital between visits to her family and friends (I assume, many of them).

This lady of seventy-three, with the perpetual smile and interest in everything and in everyone has only one lung, has survived cancer and two heart attacks. We all know positive people like this lady. They bring sunshine into our lives, and are a source of inspiration whenever we are depressed.

A sedentary acquaintance insists that friendships, such as I describe, seem very superficial to her. That's one point of view, but I can assure you that when I meet some of my newly acquired friends, the joy I feel, the warmth generated by our hugs, are almost as comforting to me, as encounters with my long time friends.

Forty years ago I realized one thing. When I gave birth to Pierre, my first baby, my heart was full of love for him. Then came Louise and, sure enough, I loved her as much as I loved Pierre. Daniel, my third baby came, and I had as much love for him as for Louise and Pierre. . . . It seems there is always room in our hearts for more children and the same is true, I think, for friends. The emotions generated by newly acquired friendships and the freedom of my nomad life do compensate somewhat for the separation from my family. We can never have everything.

CHAPTER 10

What Is a Normal Everyday Life Like?

One Typical Day

The morning sky is on fire with the orange sun rising from behind the Chocolate Mountains. The first rays pierce the cool air and sneak their way into the bedroom through half-open curtains. The light and warmth wake us up slowly. All is peaceful; no noise disturbs our languorous awakening, no schedule hurries it. We stay in bed, enjoying the moments with no worry about time, tranquil in our "little cabin" on the shore of the Salten Sea in California. It's February 1983.

Finally, I pull myself out of bed; I am hungry. I make coffee; Lucien, my husband, joins me and we eat breakfast while observing the fishermen through the picture window. They have been there for awhile; it's already ten o'clock!

As I go to sit in the sun with a book, a car pulls up. The couple greets me and says they spotted the Escapee club emblem on our RV and decided to come and meet us. Immediately we hug each other—a friendly custom of this club.

Right away, they give us two heads of lettuce they have just picked at a neighboring farm and invite us to join them and a dozen other members of the club at the Slabs, just ten miles away. It will be fun to meet these people and see old friends, especially Bud and Jean with whom we spent some time a month earlier at the co-op private SKP campground in Lakewood, New Mexico.

We thank our visitors and agree to meet them the day after at a unique site where thousands of RVers spend their winters. All it costs to stay at the Slabs is $25 for the permit, and organized activities are even provided! But we can only stay a week because we have so many other places to go! (Yes, we have seen many places, my husband and I; and many are left for me to discover. When I talk with other nomads, when I read, I am always noting more places "not to miss" and my list is getting longer and longer.)

If you have read the previous chapters, you know that nomads spend many hours sitting side by side, admiring the scenery, while driving to a planned destination. You will also stop at many places on the way and take time to "smell the roses." You will not have to hurry. You will also spend a lot of time just outside your "house," not only appreciating the view but barbequeing and eating your meals. (Don't forget that you'll probably always be in a warm climate). You will enjoy leisure time at a beach or pool as well as many other campground activities. There will be golf, fishing, tennis and flea markets. You will be going out to eat, to play cards and to visit friends. If you have any time left, you might look at TV.

Since both man and woman of an RVing couple are retired (or on holiday) most RVers share responsibility for chores. They also tend to simplify the cooking and eat out as often as the occasion arises and their budgets allow. After all the years of duty, restrictions and responsibilities, they try to accommodate each other's tastes and liberty. Whether they are in a campground or at a club rally, each part of a couple usually feels free to participate or not in the activities.

Maurice describes the flexibility of his relationship, "If I am hungry and Evelyn is not in the RV, I fix myself something to eat for lunch. If I am at the rec hall at lunchtime, I eat at the snack bar; I know that she will not fix something and wait for me. But we do eat together at night."

Hobbies

We all know that the more interests we have, the more interesting we are to others, starting with our partners. If after all the activities I have described, you think you might be bored with nomad life, maybe you have a special interest you have long wished to pursue but have been prevented from doing so because of other priorities. As a nomad, you will have time to try it. If you don't like it, just discard it for something else. There should not be any "failure guilt" when we retire. Here are a few suggestions of hobbies that people living in an RV have found interesting:

- Amateur radio can keep you in touch with the whole world and your family and friends.
- Try new recipes.
- Practice wood or other sculpting.
- Play old songs on a portable keyboard.
- Collect stones on excursions; polish them on rainy days.
- Become a good photographer; give duplicate photos to your friends; they'll love you. If you are a good narrator, prepare a slide show.
- Purchase some good binoculars and become a bird watcher.
- Study a foreign language.
- Make original mailboxes or other wood handicrafts.
- Learn calligraphy.
- Discover your genealogy and organize a family reunion.
- Experiment with painting. Most campgrounds offer lessons.

- Make friends with a computer.
- Learn palm reading.
- Study graphology and read handwriting.
- Acquire knowledge of the stars.
- Hunt for treasures with a metal detector.
- Collect stamps, postcards, unusual bumper stickers, funny business names, signs etc.

Some special interests can take you all over America, perhaps all over the world:

- Seek out festivals and carnivals.
- Go to air shows.
- Find celebrated outdoor dramas.
- Experience all the raft trips.
- Study mushrooms.
- Visits all the Amish communities.
- Investigate restored downtowns and compare.
- . . . historic settlements,
- . . . beautiful shopping centers,
- . . . theme parks,
- . . . zoos,
- . . . famous residences,
- . . . caverns,
- . . . museums of a particular kind,
- . . . Indian villages,
- . . . cascades.
- Participate in bike tours or marathons.
- Photograph unusual architecture.
- Take part in outdoor seminars.
- Join a square dancing group and meet other groups.
- Enter shuffleboard tournaments.
- Sample regional foods.
- Register in Elderhostel courses here or abroad.

. . .and you thought you would be bored? Quite the contrary! The nomad life makes it possible to become a specialist, an authority on something new for you. With this life you have the time and the opportunity for whatever interests you.

Of course, if you join camping clubs, you will be invited to all kinds of rallies like the FMCA Rocky Mountain Ramble in conjunction with the Albuquerque International Balloon Fiesta. You will also get ideas from reading about others' travels in club magazines and newsletters.

On rainy days, there are letters to write. If you don't like to write, perhaps it is because you don't know what to say. But as a nomad, many things will be very interesting to family and friends left behind. And you will surely have some fresh information for the new friends you have made while traveling.

What about reading? Isn't that a wonderful hobby? One you can enjoy anytime? The public library is the best place to investigate a hobby. Reading is really a very captivating way to spend a rainy day or . . . any day.

When you are constantly on the move, you obviously cannot become a member of a public library, but there is another way to pick up free books wherever your travels take you. In many well organized campgrounds, there is a library section in the recreation halls. You can take books you want to read with you and replace them with books you have already read; it is a common practice and most of the time you do not have to ask permission.

There are other ways to keep busy while giving help or pleasure to others. Volunteer work will take up some of your recreational time but will give you a very satisfying feeling in return. Sitting and talking around is another very popular hobby with RVers. It pays to take time to listen to others and to care for each other. Everyone needs to be appreciated.

CHAPTER 11

How Much Does the Nomad Lifestyle Cost?

A Few Nomads Give the Facts

How much does the nomad lifestyle cost? It is the first question asked by people about this way of life. I understand their concern; it's so different from life in a regular house. But one thing is certain: it's cheaper. . . . All full-time nomads agree on this.

It's impossible to give an annual cost estimate because the thousands of nomads enjoy many variations of this life. However, after reading this book, you will be able to figure out how much it will cost you, according to what kind of life on wheels you choose. Right now, at home, your expenses are probably very different from those of your neighbor, although his house is probably similar to yours. The same applies to the nomads. Each chooses an RV and lifestyle according to budget and tastes.

Ed and Helen live year around in an eighteen foot travel trailer. Ed understands mechanics and repairs his own car; he enjoys it and saves quite a lot of money doing his own work. He also likes fishing and spends a lot of time doing it; this results in savings also. He and Helen like to pick their own fruits and vegetables along their travel routes; they get better quality and more for their money and it's good exercise. Helen makes preserves and jams. They buy little clothing or anything else; and when they do, they patronize Salvation Army stores and the like. Helen makes all the gifts they give friends and family. They eat in a restaurant only to celebrate an anniversary. They are clean, good company and hospitable. Of course, they do not serve scotch to their guests, but iced tea does nicely. They enjoy spending each day near a river or close to the sea, and at nights park in a shopping center or other free space. Once in a while they go to a low priced public campground to service their RV systems.

This couple used to lead a normal life: As a retired security officer, Ed gets only $600 per month from his retirement fund. Helen was a secretary, but she is younger and does not get a pension yet. They much prefer living the way they do to freezing on the way to work up north, paying a large portion of their income to heat an apartment, and being no richer. Helen is very happy; she has very little housekeeping to do and has all the time in the world to indulge in her passions, reading and traveling. They both intend to live like this for the rest of their lives.

The other side of the coin is represented by Bill and Joan, who live in a $350,000 motorhome. They tow a car, but not just any car—it's a Mercedes. They own a water-front condo RV lot in California, for which they must have paid at least $60,000. They spend a lot of time there during the winter on a thirty-eight foot cruiser. During the summer, they travel all over to play the best golf clubs. They go to the racetracks, follow the nightclub circuit and prefer restaurants with ambiance. Understandably, they stop only at the most beautiful campgrounds. Bill says money was made to be spent, and they want to make the best of what they have for whatever time is left to them on this earth.

I personally am situated somewhere between these two extremes. The more you read about the different types of RV life and travel, services, available activities and fees, the better you will understand the income you will require as a nomad to accommodate your tastes and what you need to be comfortable.

In 1983 Frank and Ann told me that they were spending $1,600 per month because that's what they were getting every month, however they were sure they could manage with much less. They spent everything they were receiving and didn't want to save for their golden years like so many others at 65; these were their golden years and they were smart enough to enjoy them.

Some Figures

When you first start this life, it's as if you are on vacation. You spend money almost without limit, visit all the museums and attractions and purchase souvenirs for everyone. In time, you don't visit so many museums, only those that you prefer; you're not attracted to all the theme parks and shows, only the very unusual ones. You begin to seek out the unknown, the different. You will always find strange places to discover and you will always marvel at man's accomplishments. But, as you become more discriminating, you save money. The same thing is true with gifts you purchase; after noticing what the recipients of your mementos have done with them, you save money by not purchasing gifts for others so frequently.

Vehicle Expenses

Repairs for the same car might cost more if done by an unknown garage. Repairs on a truck, van or motorhome cost

more in general. Add 15 to 30% to your actual car maintenance costs. You will probably travel greater distances with
your RV so you can expect higher maintenance costs. That is
why many RVers become amateur mechanics. Most nomads
change their own oil, etc.

Telephone

No phone service or installation fees are necessary for the
nomad. On the other hand, he might pay for a cellular phone
or a message service and occasional long distance calls. With
no such service, (Chapter 8) he has to make many toll calls to
"report" to people who cannot reach him. Here, the extra
money he spends depends on actual use of the telephone
and in what way it will change. Some people always write
and seldom phone.

Groceries

Your meal costs might be a little bit more because you will
probably buy wherever you happen to be; even if you save
coupons and buy at the same chain, you will not buy in
quantity. This is one habit that is hard to leave behind; saving
money by buying in quantity is out unless you want to
overweigh your cupboards with canned food or clutter every
corner of the RV with stored paper products. (I have seen
this quite often). Remember that being on the road, you can
always pick up what you need at a convenience store adja-
cent to a gas station or at a campground store. The simplicity
is well worth the few pennies. You want an easy life, don't
you? You buy fewer groceries because you eat at restaurants
more often; you pass in front of them all the time and they're
very tempting!

Clothing

You will probably spend less on clothing than you presently budget. First, if you're a northener, you can forget about fur coats, boots and all winter clothes. Second, the people around you will change all the time, so what you wear is new to them! Thirdly, your life will be simpler; you'll need only one dressy outfit; most of the time you will be in casual clothes, mainly mix and match. There is no room for dozens of pairs of shoes and handbags, only a few in one basic color.

Postal Expenses

The cost of postage will be determined by how many gifts or letters to your loved ones you send and how many magazines, club newsletters and pieces of personal correspondence you receive (See Chapter 8.).

Entertainment

The cost of tickets to attractions and museums will probably compare with what you spend now for concerts and the theater. As for having friends for dinner, there is a *tendency* among all RVers to eat out instead, with each paying his own bill.

Insurance

Insuring your RVing unit will probably cost you about the same as insuring your house and car combined. Your personal insurance will be the same, but you might have to add travel insurance.

Fuel

To estimate the difference in your fuel costs, you must consider the amount you presently spend for going back and forth to work, shopping, visiting friends and what you now spend on vacations for gas or air tickets, restaurants and motels (See Chapter 1). You will not have any of these expenses, traveling in an RV. On the other hand, your fuel costs in an RV will depend on whether you travel everyday, drive 50 or 75 m.p.h. or stay put for weeks on end.

Campground Fees

If you prefer to stay in nice campgrounds every traveling day, it can cost an average of $20 a day or $600 a month. If you usually park where it costs nothing and you go to a nice campground once a week, it will cost you an average of $80 a month, a very low rent indeed! (See Chapter 3.).

But most people will probably choose the middle ground. You can find campgrounds with a pool and all kinds of recreation for $300 a month. So, you can travel from one such location to another, spending one month at each, even in different states. If you sell your house, and put the money in the bank, even if you deduct the price of the RV, the interest on the balance will more than cover your monthly rent. The total cost of maintaining a house is probably more than this! So, if you want to roam around and change your surroundings once in a while, you probably can do it, and you might still have enough to take a cruise or to join a European caravan once in a while.

A Low Cost Example

To help you even more, look at the scenario of a happy RV life with a little traveling on only $15,000 a year. It is possible.

You can pull a trailer with a car and go south, let's say, to the Texan Valley. On your way down, you stop at suggested free spots overnight and visit a few places that sound interesting. Then you rent a lot in a nice campground for six months. You make lots of friends, participate in most activities and take two side trips for five days each. Then, after saying goodbye, you go back north along another route, and visit some more places.

Up north, you rent a lot in a nice campground for six months, perhaps close to where you have friends and family and once in awhile, you visit them and park in front of their houses. Other times, they come and visit you in your campground, using the pool. You can make friends. After six months, you say goodbye and go south to the same campground where you were the previous winter, using another road, in order to see some more sights. Or, you go to another state to see something different and you choose a nice campsite. . . . Not too bad a life for $15,000 a year. . . .

An estimate of what your costs would be follows. Remember these figures are approximate and may have to be adjusted to a higher cost of living in the future:

Texas campground fees for 6 months	$ 1,200.
Electricity	120.
Propane for 12 months	180.
Northern camp fees for the other 6 months (incl. electricity)	1,000.
Insurance for low cost car & trailer	400.
Personal & medical insurance	1,500.
Food for two incl. restaurant meals	5,200.
Clothing	600.
Gifts, telephone calls, mail	200.
Shows, attractions	200.
Camp fees in transit	160.
Car & RV maintenance	600.

Gas (10,000 miles at 10 to a gallon)   1,000.
Miscellaneous ($220 × 12 months)   2,640.

                                    TOTAL $15,000.

Maybe you would rather travel more. You can, even on $15,000! You can boondock most of the time along your traveling routes instead of staying put in a campground for months and use what you would pay for campground fees for the extra gas you will need. It's your choice. Maybe you do not have an income of $15,000. You can trade services or work along the way. (See Chapter 1)

Of course, you can spend much more. If, for instance, you live in a coach and pull an expensive car, your insurance will be much more. And so will your fuel cost. If you take a cruise and two organized RV trips in foreign countries each year, you've added $20,000 to your yearly expenses. If you try all the best golf courses and the best restaurants, it adds quite a few thousand dollars, especially if you spend your evenings at the best shows or at the races, instead of playing cards and shuffleboard at a campground and eating at the local low price buffets with other RVers.

It is obvious that fulltime RVers have more leeway in their budgets than those who live in a house. It's certainly an easier life for retirees than trying to maintain the same house as they did before their incomes were reduced by retirement.

CHAPTER 12

How Do You Choose a Residence Vehicle?

Trailer or Motorhome?

One of the first questions asked by people who are curious about RVing is which is best, a trailer or a motorhome? There is no consensus among experienced RVers; it is the eternal discussion. It depends entirely on how you will live in your RV. After reading about all the different ways you can live the nomad life, you should now know pretty well what your style will be.

Here are the questions you should ask yourself:

• For how many people will the RV be home?
• Do I like to entertain for dinner or to play games?
• Do I plan to have overnight guests?
• Do I have a hobby that takes a lot of space?
• Do I need space to store articles I will be selling?
• Do I want to keep my car or truck?
• Am I going to be stationary most of the time?

- If I stay put for only a few days at a time, will I want to go out (shopping, to shows and restaurants) everyday?
- Do I like to be on the move most of the time, transporting everything I own with me?

As for me, since I answered yes to numbers 2, 3, 4, and 9, and am just one person, I chose a twenty-two-foot mini-motorhome. It would also be good for two people with not much hobby or sports paraphernalia. I use the bed in the back and my overnight guests sleep in the bunk above the cab which leaves the dinette as dining/living room space between the two "bedrooms." This RV is small enough so that I can park it almost anywhere. And since I like to follow my whims, it's good to have everything with me all the time. When I'm on my way from one place to another, and decide to go somewhere else, I can just keep going giving me the ultimate sense of freedom.

Of course, if I know I am camping only a day or two, I might choose not to open the awning, not to connect the water, etc. I keep everything tied down, so that nothing breaks. I don't carry plants and I keep things where they belong, so I am always ready to go in minutes, if I want to.

But, if you'd rather stay put for awhile, with the use of all that makes an RV a home, you might want to buy a longer motorhome and tow a car or other extra transportation (See Chapter 2), or buy a trailer and use the towing unit for day trips. It could be a van, a big car or a truck to tow a trailer, or a flatbed truck to tow a fifth-wheeler.

Having a truck you want to keep might not be the only reason you would want to choose a travel trailer. Most twenty-seven foot trailers have a closed bedroom in the back (double bed or twins), a dinette in the center, and a sofa with folding table in the front. To have the same arrangement in a motorhome, you would have to buy a thirty-three foot one, which would cost quite a bit more than a trailer. Another advantage of a trailer is that you can tow it with a van with sleeping and eating facilities that are convenient for short fishing trips, etc. You may ask why buy a motorhome and tow a car? Some people do not like to tow a long trailer and they like the convenience of having access to their "house" while on the road. If it's raining when you stop, you don't have to go outside.

If, however you're not comfortable towing a long trailer, you could buy a fifth wheeler and tow it with a flat bed truck. The interior offers a bi-level floor plan with a larger bathroom. The manner in which a fifth wheel is hitched to the truck creates an overlap in the two vehicles and reduces total tow vehicle-trailer length. The turning radius, with its centered pivot point, often is tighter than that of a similar length tow vehicle travel trailer configuration with better maneuverability as a result. The pick-up truck can be used as a camper pick-up.

There is such a variety of vehicles and combinations available that it is impossible to make recommendations. Do not overlook the micro-mini-motorhomes which are smaller and not as powerful but require less gas. But you must remember that you will be spending many waking hours in your "home on wheels." Think of the rainy days when you may have company or when you're sick; space and comfort are very important, especially if there will be two people or more. Buy a vehicle as big as you can afford; I say, compromise the least possible on size. It might make the difference between liking RVing or not, particularly if one partner is not too enthusiastic about the idea. However, remember that the longer the RV is, the more you are limited by places to park; some campgrounds cannot accept RV's larger than 30 feet. And, fuel costs are greater for a larger vehicle.

Don't begin saying, "We'll start with a small one to see if we're going to like living in an RV." It's better to buy secondhand, if you can't afford a new RV of the size you want, or if you are wary of this life or the type of RV you are choosing. If you decide to change or sell a new RV the year after purchase, you will surely lose money. If, on the other hand, you have a clean older RV that you purchased for a bargain price, you probably will not lose much money. If you're contemplating buying a motorhome and towing a car, you must consider the cost of owning and operating a car, the money invested and interest lost, devaluation and insurance, registration, and maintenance costs. It is not exact to look at the odometer and say, like many RVers, "All this mileage with my big machine would have cost me much more in gas!" What happens is that with a car, you always go from A to B, and come back to A (your motorhome), or eat out. If you use your motorhome most of the time wherever you go, as I do now, and as my husband and I used to do with our 30-foot motorhome, you save mileage and overnight expenses that you must pay when you leave your motorhome behind. "What about the constant bother disconnecting and rolling up the awning?" people ask me. . . . It takes just ten minutes to disconnect and twenty to settle back. We have plenty of time . . . there's no rush.

I keep a running list of things, groceries, etc., I need, and before I settle in at a campground, I buy what I need. Many campgrounds have a grocery store anyway. When I really want to see a city, I take a tour. It's not expensive and more relaxing. Once in a while I leave my mini at a parking area and use a subway; or I leave it where there is free parking and take a bus or a cab. It is possible to save much money by not towing a car.

With the new motorhomes, there is a lot of storage space underneath and you can always install some pods for extra storage capacity on the sturdy roof. You can also use the roof for a sundeck or a box seat at football games, etc.

The new taller RVs do have one disadvantage. There are not many garages with roofs high enough to accommodate them when they need repairs; but, when you do find one, the mechanic might let you remain inside your vehicle, so that you can write a letter, take a shower, etc. You might even get permission to stay overnight.

Before you make a definite decision about what type of RV you might want, trailer or motorhome, you need to compare the price difference between the two types of the same length. Study the pages of a RV buyer guide and whenever you have the opportunity, go to an RV dealer and compare models. Ask your dealer when and where there will be an RV show, so you can see a variety of brands and models.

When you think you have found the ideal layout for your RV living, consider the following:

- Is the height of the ceiling comfortable for you or your tall friends?
- Is the dinette table wide enough to accommodate four people for dinner?
- Remove your shoes and enter the shower; it won't be as wide as the one in a house, but is it too low and/or too cramped?
- Is the bed long enough and wide enough for you?
- Is the sofabed comfortable to sleep on? easy to open? When open, does it leave room to walk around? Is it relatively comfortable to sit on?
- Sit on all the chairs; does the passenger chair have sufficient room for feet?
- Can you tie down the TV set in a place where you will be comfortable watching it in your accustomed position?

Personally, if I had to choose between a sofa and a dinette, I would prefer the dinette if wide. Four people can sit comfortably face to face for conversation; better than four in a row on a sofa. Besides being practical for dinner guests and game players, it gives you a place to open a newspaper or study a map. You can use it to do an occasional piece of ironing on top of a blanket, instead of carrying an ironing board. It is totally necessary if you want to write or pursue any hobby.

A sofa is usually offered with a narrow removable table that is a bother to set up at every mealtime. You may have to make up a bed every night, if you choose between a sofa and a bed or a dinette and a bed. You'll probably have to make some choices when you purchase a medium or small RV.

When shopping for an RV, try to be aware of inconveniences that would become annoying which could not be corrected. Sit on the toilet (I'm not kidding) to make certain there is enough space at the sides and front. Lie down on the beds to check their sizes and to determine if any cabinet at the foot of the bed will bother you. Don't dismiss an RV if you like everything but the mattresses; a factory or the dealer can replace them. While you're "in bed," if there's no night tables, look for a place to add a shelf on which you can put a glass, a book, or your eyeglasses. You can mount a light on the wall. These things will be important, should you be sick in bed.

Open all the drawers and cabinets; some might be fake or very small.

One last suggestion to help you buy the right "home on wheels." Join Escapees Club right away, even if you don't have an RV at the present. The information you will receive about fulltime life on the road will be invaluable. And, you will be invited to the next Escapade where you can attend seminars on every subject, including "How to Select the Right RV."

Then you can call the large RV renting organizations and try their Fly/Rent an RV deals. You will have both a useful and fun holiday.

Features and Equipment

Even a small RV must have two used water tanks, one for the black water and one for the gray water and no amount of gray water should go into the black water tank, otherwise it will fill too fast. Make sure by checking the diagram included with the user's manual or check the pipes underneath.

I once parked a new mini-motorhome in my daughter's driveway. Around eleven o'clock at night, we were chattering in front of the house, when I decided to let out the gray water. After all, there was nothing wrong with it since it would flow down the street drain. I pulled the key and. . . . what a disaster! The black water tank was emptying itself! I still can see my son-in-law's astonished face under the street light! My daughter ran to get the hose and to flush the toilet paper and all off the asphalt and out of sight down the street drain. Can you imagine a more embarrassing moment?

That night, I set the alarm clock to make sure I woke up at six o'clock the next morning. I hosed off the driveway again and sprinkled it with a lot of detergent; at seven I repeated the operation. I had to make sure everything was impeccable and without odor. . . . my daughter was having a garage sale at eight o'clock that morning!

What had happened was that I had just exchanged my big motorhome for a new mini and had never thought, not one moment, that the gray water tank could not be located on the same side as my big motorhome.

Even in a campground for any length of time always leave the black water tank closed until you are ready to empty it so that the water rushes out forcefully and nothing dries in the sewer pipe. Leave the gray water tank open so that water from the sink and shower runs out as you use it. Shortly before it's time to empty the black water, close the gray water valve and accumulate some gray water. Then, you proceed like you would do anytime you want to empty at a dumping station, empty the black water, close the valve, then open the gray water tank so the sewer tube is rinsed out. Close the valve, remove the tube and proceed on your way.

One feature that you may like in some motorhomes is jalousie windows. If you have the standard sliding windows, you'll probably want to install awnings so that you can leave the windows open when it rains. You may want to buy a roof vent cover for the same reason.

After you have found a layout that you like, ask the dealer to show you all the equipment and how it functions. (Go during the week because the parttime weekend sales people may not know much.) Try to talk with the dealer in person and ask for a brochure that will list all the extras and features for the sake of making comparisons in the future.

One convenience that I find really essential is electronic controls on the inside for the water heater, the refrigerator and the furnace. The dealer can install them. A motorhome needs an automotive air conditioner to keep you cool when you are driving, even if you have a roof air-conditioning unit.

It is a wise precaution to buy a gas detector. If you smell cooking cabbage or old garbage, *beware!* Check the gas tank, it could be only because it's almost empty. If not, there must be a gas leak. (To be on the safe side, always leave a small window open.) Check all the seams, connections and valves of the stove first and then of all the gas lines. Use a paintbrush to dab on some soapy water. If you see bubbles, there is a leak, and you must tighten the connection. If you cannot correct the situation, immediately turn off the valve at the tank.

If you plan to spend much time in a cold climate, the standard RV heater may use too much current to go "boon-docking." (see Chapter 2) The best thing is to buy a catalytic heater. Some require 12v only to be activated, and all run on very little propane, making much less noise than a standard furnace since they have no fan. But remember, if your standard heater does draw too much from the battery, you can always turn on your engine for a while to recharge it.

In order to prevent water lines from breaking, install a pressure regulator at the tap, or leave the tap partially open. You can also install a water purifier at the water entry of an

RV if you are concerned about excess mineral content affecting your health and tanks and water lines.

An RV usually comes with a hose, but you should buy a second one to connect with a Y at the water faucet. This second hose is handy to wash the car, put out a camp fire or take an outside shower.

To make sure every electric connection that you may want to use gives you the right current, buy a small portable voltage indicator; use it especially prior to turning on your roof air conditioner or anything else, it will save you much money on repairs.

A good TV antenna is necessary; a dish is better. You might want a closed circuit TV to monitor the area outside your motorhome as well as electronic jacks; this is not necessary, but nice to have. A awning at the entrance of your RV is a "must," as well as a piece of outdoor carpet, folding chairs and table, and a portable barbeque and Voilâ! Your instant patio!

If you decide to buy a travel trailer or a fifth-wheeler, don't forget to check its weight with that which the tow vehicle can safely pull before you finalize the purchase of one or the other. It is very important not only the vehicles' weights match correctly, but that you use a swaybar and that your hitching system is secure. The tow vehicle *must* be equipped adequately. Read the brochures suggested in the appendix, and see a large dealership that sells trailers or go to a U-Haul that services RVs and get more information. Do all this before buying a tow vehicle; the truck salesman might not know for sure what equipment you require.

Security

Chapter 3 discussed certain security measures that nomads must take. There is equipment that can be added to an RV that may increase your peace of mind, although it's very

improbable that it will be needed. If you have sliding windows, you can use sticks in the tracks to prevent their being
opened. A burglar alarm system is available which has its
own battery; it has a delayed reaction that allows you time to
disconnect it when you do not want it to go off. You can also
install a panic-button alarm, which you press if you want
attention because you feel unsafe.

To help police locate you or your stolen RV, you can paint
identification numbers on your roof. If they are large enough
(4 feet), a police helicopter will be able to locate your RV from
the air. You can buy these numbers; they're called RV-ID. You
can engrave a code on your articles of value (police usually
provide engraving tools). Keep a list of your coded items and
give a copy of it and the numbers on your roof to a family
member or friend.

A portable CB is important because it enables you to communicate with other RVers or call for help. There are hundreds of additional articles and gadgets you can add to your
RV. After you receive your first issue of *Camping World,* you'll
probably be like a kid looking at a toy catalog.

Purchasing a Pre-owned RV

The styles change in RV models just like in everything else.
Before buying new you will find it interesting to compare the
colors and different layouts of older RVs. RVs that are only
five years old or so will not be very different, but the price is.

If you find one that you like, you should check certain
things. You will know right away if leaks are a problem.
When you smell mildew, forget the unit. Look for stains on
the ceiling, the walls, around the lights, the switches, and
windows. If in doubt, examine the roof; if you see many
coats of silicon on some spots or if there are storage pods,
that could explain the stains; there must be water coming in
somewhere. With a flashlight, check the inside of the cabinets and closets. Check the waterline, starting at the electric

pump, and all along and around the sinks and the toilet base. The wood could be rotten.

Check the RV systems too. Have the compression and the transmission checked by a good mechanic. Ask the seller for the owner's guide or write to the manufacturer.

RV rental companies are good sources of used motor-homes for sale.

Renting an RV

Before you buy an RV, you might be wise to rent first. It is rather expensive but worth it if it prevents you from making a mistake. Check the RV rentals section in the Appendix and try to rent one similar to the one you would like to buy. Many RVers trade a motorhome for a trailer, then a van, then a. . . . which is all right for someone with money to spare.

Choosing a Dealer

Although most RV dealers are honest, you need to be on your guard. There are dealers who will charge extra for features that should be included if they can get away with it. They can then advertize the unit at a price lower than the competition. If he is not honest in this way, he will probably also bill you for work that is covered by warranty. He may pretend to be able to repair something he cannot, or he may refuse to repair what is under the warranty.

Some people have bought an RV, paid cash or given a deposit, and instructed a dealer to inspect it or make adjustments, if needed. Two days later, when they are all excited about picking up their new vehicle, the salesman tells them there was a mistake in the contract, amounting to $1,000 or more. People may be so enthusiastic about having the RV that they agree to pay the extra $1,000 without too much thought.

I heard of a couple from Minnesota, who made an unfortunate choice of dealer even though they were shopping for their eighth RV. They saw a mini-motorhome of the year, with only 950 miles on it, at an unfamiliar dealer located in another town, and bought it. They were promised the warranty papers, but they never received them. Then they discovered that it was not an authorized dealer for this brand, so he was not bound to respect the warranty. When they went to get some adjustments and repairs done, the business had been closed by the police, for fraud. They learned that many of the RVs left there on consignment had been rented or sold without the owners' knowledge. Even experienced RVers can be taken.

It's better to deal with a reputable business in the town where you live; it will be more convenient in the long run. Investigate the repair shop and talk to the RV owners waiting for their vehicles. If the shop is not well equipped or the customers are unhappy, beware. And later, if the dealer you've chosen does not give you satisfaction, file a complaint with the manufacturer.

Financing an RV

There are now quite a variety of ways to finance an RV. A dealer will probably offer a loan through his bank or with the manufacturer's acceptance corporation, which is the current trend in RV loans. Just as Ford Motor Credit Corporation offers consumer financing for its company's products, some RV makers have similar programs.

Before you sign a contract with a dealer, investigate other sources for loans to make certain you are getting the best financing deal. Before you even start looking, you should write to the Good Sam Club for information on their RV Financing. FMCA also has a plan, but only for Class A, Class C and bus conversions. Your own bank may also have reasonable loans for recreational vehicles. If you know all these options, you will be able to make the right choice.

Insuring an RV

A variety of insurance coverage is available for RVs. Contact Good Sam for all RVs, Coast-to-Coast for all RVs, FMCA for motorhomes, Alexander & Alexander for motorhomes, Caravanner Insurance for travel trailers, Foremost Insurance for staionary RVs and special trip insurance if you move it and RVA Insurance for travel trailers only. In addition, you should consult your own insurance broker.

Should You Be a Motorhome Landlord?

Some dealers have a plan whereby they will rent out your motorhome when you're not using it. You might have thought of doing it on your own . . . if you're not ready yet to live in it fulltime. First, consider the age and mechanical condition of your RV. If you rent a 1975 motorhome to someone who neglects to add that extra quart of oil every 200 miles, your vehicle won't last long and you might receive an angry call at 2 o'clock in the morning from a stranded family. Consider how dependable and maintenance-free your RV is. Then check your insurance coverage with your agent. Check also the warranty coverage. The fact that someone else is driving your vehicle may alter your coverage.

Another problem is to determine how much to charge. Call a few of the agencies in the yellow pages to find out what area RV rental companies charge. You might base your fee on a little less: so much per week with 1,000 miles free and a flat per mile rate for anything more.

You should require a deposit—maybe $300—for possible damage. Check over your RV with the renter and make a list of the actual dents and other damage for future reference; explain how the equipment functions to make sure nothing is broken as a result of ignorance.

A written agreement is a must, in case a legal problem later arises. A standard motorhome rental form can be obtained from Jenkins Business Forms. A lease form is also recommended. Help the tenant take care of your RV by lending him the owner's manual. Tape a card with a notation of the height of the vehicle on the dash, along with a reminder to lower the TV antenna. Lend him this book.

Before making the decision to become a motorhome landlord, figure all the costs: advertizing, extra mechanical checkups, carpet cleaning, etc. It is a lot of bother.

CHAPTER 13

Making an RV Your Home

You have probably chosen a particular RV because you liked its layout and found it convenient. But however perfect it was when you bought it, you will want to make additions and perhaps some transformations in order to feel more at home. We all know that there is never enough space in an RV to store everything we own. I hope you started working on this problem after reading Chapter 11 and you have reduced your wardrobe as well as the number of your mementos. But little by little as you enter this lifestyle, you will acquire all kinds of things, brochures about clubs and trips, maps, books about RVs and about your hobbies, etc. Mom may like to knit and sew—the notions and fabrics take space; and Dad may collect stamps—he needs some space too.

So, if you need more storage space, go through every little corner, every empty space and consider how you could make it usable. There might be a few inches space under the closet floor, and certainly behind your hanging clothes there is room for a shoe bag in which you could organize things you do not use all the time. You can use shoebags anywhere you can hang them to store breakable items. If your closet is wide enough, you could hang shirts and other short clothing on one side and use the space underneath for shelves or for items you want to pile up. Plastic dishpans make good drawers.

Under the mattress, there might be a board over empty space; detach it and secure it with hinges and you have an extra chest. You may even be able to provide access to such a space from outside by making an opening between the joists and attaching a retrofit door available through RV dealers. The indoor steps can be hinged to provide access to space for storing tools or shoes. Under the kitchen sink there may be room to add an extra shelf if you re-arrange the pipes. But don't forget to store heavy items on the floor so they will not do damage in the event that you need to brake hard while in transit.

There are never enough shelves in the cabinets; some RVs have no shelves at all. When you have decided where you want to put what (I change my mind about ten times), you can divide your cabinet space. For instance, you can put a shelf over the cups (I personally find the shelves made like a bench very useful because you can move them whenever your needs change. Cover the shelves with carpeting or foam so the dishes don't slide. I use the rectangular plastic dish pans for organizing cabinets which are hard to reach. They are easy to grab for short people like me, and keep your belongings classified.

Instead of folding your clothes, roll them; they will be less wrinkled. Use magazine racks that are sold in RV stores on the walls; they can store writing paper and many other items neatly. In department stores, you can find plastic containers of all shapes; afix them on the wall to store your eyeglasses by the bed, your combs by the bathroom sink, the shampoo by the shower, etc.

Outside, you could add a box between the body of the RV

and the bumper. You can either build it or buy it at an RV store. It will be useful to store folding bicycles, your lawn chairs, hoses, leveling blocks, etc. By thoroughly inspecting your RV, inside, outside and underneath, you will probably find other empty spaces you can adapt for storage.

Clothes and Their Care

It's all very well to add storage space, but the key to comfortable RV living is to first reduce what you carry. Select clothes in a basic color scheme. You will need open and closed shoes, high heels and flats. You will have room for about a dozen pairs of shoes—that's six pairs apiece if there are two of you. Stay away from white clothing that needs bleach. Not only do you want to reduce the volume, you want to reduce the work! It is best to have sheets, towels and dishtowels in a dark color. You should have enough dark clothes for a machine load. And you really don't want anything that requires ironing. As far as I am concerned, the new fashionable cotton, silk and linen is taking us back thirty-five years to the time we were slaves to the ironing board. Unless you really perspire, you don't need to throw a T-shirt in the laundry basket after wearing it only a few hours; you can wear it again unless you've spilled your lunch on it. If you have dozens of socks and underwear they're washed in the machine. Or, you can wash them by hand everyday if you're used to that, but think of the water you'll spend if you boondock.

When I first started doing my wash in laundromats, one thing I didn't like was not being able to shorten the washing machine cycles. But there is always a good side to everything; if I have three loads, I can use three washing machines at the same time. If my RV is parked right in front of the laundry, I can make the bed, take a shower or write a letter. When the operation is completed, I immediately put all the clothes back in their places before I move on to something more interesting. Some nomads prefer to wash by hand, but check campground rules before you hang up clothes outside to dry. A good way to wash a few clothes is to put them in soapy water in a covered sink or pail while you're traveling. The vehicle in motion will agitate the clothes, and when you stop, all you have to do is rinse them and hang them up on a dryer that attaches to the back of your RV.

Once in a while, you will need to press something for a special occasion, so you don't always look like a camper. Just use a folded blanket or beach towel on the dinette table instead of an ironing board.

Try to keep everything simple; only two bed sheet sets and towel sets and the minimum of hand towels and dishtowels are necessary. If you have weekend guests, ask them to bring sleeping bags and towels. As much as possible, use every item for at least two functions. For instance, I use my portable electric oven for a toaster and my dough-mixing bowl to serve salads and potato chips. The removable part of the garbage can I use for a pail.

House Cleaning

There are ways to reduce the number of cleaning products you carry. Toothpaste can clean your jewelry, remove dark streaks from a floor and mildew stains from a shower curtain. White vinegar mixed with water deodorizes a kitchen counter and gets rid of the ants. Vinegar in rinse water cuts through soap residue; use it half and half with water to wash windows and mirrors. To prolong the life of cut flowers, put them in one quart of lukewarm water to which you have added two teaspoons of vinegar and three tablespoons of sugar. Even a cat benefits from vinegar; one teaspoon in its drinking water discourages fleas.

Baking soda is good for many different things; write for an Arm & Hammer pamphlet.

Arranging Your Belongings

When you place your belongings in an RV, you must think of the weight; it has to be distributed so that the heavier articles are in front over the axles. Everything that can fall down must be tied up. I use bungies (elastic cords with a hook at each end which come different lengths) to secure my TV, my electric oven and my garbage can to the wall. All bottles I place in an empty soda carton so they don't rattle and break.

To make sure that I always secure my TV I just found a good trick: I hang a little Mexican hat on the bungie cord (of course, any trinquet will do). When I take the bungie off the TV, I hang the hat on my shifting stick. Whenever I'm ready to drive away, the little hat reminds me to secure the TV and to lower the antenna.

While paying attention to weight and things that could fall, you need to think about making the best use of the limited space. There is a logical place for everything; there is no use in carrying something that you can't find when you need it. It is not easy at first; everyone, like me, changes the arrangement many times. After all, it's not like moving from a house to another house, where closets, cabinets and drawers are more or less in the same place. In fact, you will probably have almost no drawers. So, reorganize, be systematic and most of all always put things back where they belong.

In the Kitchen

An RV kitchen called "galley" can very easily become overcrowded. Keep only those utensils and pots and pans you absolutely cannot do without; only one set of unbreakable dishes is necessary and they can go in the microwave. There are fancy "cut glass" plastic glasses you can throw away, perfectly acceptable for a dinner party as long as you don't forget the unbreakable candlesticks, candles and the colorful napkins matching the wash and wear placemats.

On Boondocking Days

"How do you make toast when you have no 110v for your toaster?" There is a special grill to use over a gas burner. I use it also under pans to keep food at "simmer" temperature. To open cans don't bother with an electric can opener, it just takes space. I have two manual key openers (in case one breaks), the simple ones with the big key that turns easily.

I also have many appliances that work either on 12v, or butane or with small batteries: a TV, radio, typewriter, cassette recorder, portable keyboard, hair dryer and hair curling iron. There is always something new on the market to make the RV life even more comfortable in these fully self-sufficient homes.

One day I was parked at my son Pierre's house and was plugged into his house power when a blackout occurred in the city. It was autumn and rather chilly by late afternoon. My son worried that I would be cold and uncomfortable in the dark. He wanted me to come into his house! It was quite funny. I thanked him and said, "You're more in trouble than I am; everything runs on 110 volts at your place. Here, I just have to switch my fridge to propane, light my propane heater if I'm cold, make dinner for you on my propane range, and I even have room enough so the five of you can sleep here. As for the lighting, as you see, there is no problem with the 12v system." He accepted my invitation and laughing went back to his house to gather the family.

The electric current came back half an hour later and, instead of having their visit, which would have pleased me a lot, Pierre and his family insisted that I have dinner at their house, once more. . . . And once more, it was very nice to be together.

Chapter 14

How Do You Drive an RV?

Advantages

Many people tell me they could never live as I do, simply because they hate to drive. I too, at one time, did not really like to drive. But, as a real estate agent, I had to drive everyday. Then I helped my husband drive to our vacation destinations. We had to leave early in the morning and drove many miles the first day, stopping early to be sure to find a motel room, eat at a decent place (if there was one), unpack, pack again, and on and on. We had to be sure to be at our destination on a specific date because of our reservations and the limited time we had for a vacation. It was the same scenario on the way home. Stress, stress and more stress. Driving was surely not a pleasure for me in those days.

Things are not at all the same if you lead a nomadic life. Now, I really enjoy driving. I go where I want, when I want, and with all the comforts of my little home. Sitting high in a motorhome or in the van that pulls a trailer, you have a much more secure feeling than in a car. You can see far in front of you; you can see the water when you cross a bridge because the parapet top is not at your eye level anymore. Having your motel and restaurant with you plus all the time in the world gives you such a feeling of freedom that driving becomes a pleasure, an escape. You would love it!

Practice

Before you take off on your first trip in a new RV, go to a deserted shopping center parking lot and practice handling the vehicle. If you are pulling a trailer, as long as you go straight forward, the trailer will follow the vehicle it is pulled by. Turning a corner is another matter. The trailer will require more space when turning, as will a motorhome.

To determine how much space you will require to make a turn, mark down with chalk an imaginary road twelve feet wide. If you turn on a right angle, you will probably use eighteen feet with an eighteen foot motorhome and about twenty-two feet (ten feet extending into the other lane) with a thirty-foot motorhome. You will need to take a partner with you to trace the arc your vehicle requires.

Then try backing up. In a motorhome you do it the same way as with a car, but visibility is not as good. It is recommended that you use a plastic fresno lens on your rear window; it increases your field of vision and helps you to see anything behind you; it is the only way you can see what is on the pavement directly behind the car unless you have a special closed circuit TV.

With a trailer, when you back up to the right, you must turn the steering wheel to the left. A little trick of the trade is to grasp the bottom of the steering wheel with one hand; that hand should move in the direction you want your trailer to go. Remember, if you have a trailer with only one axle, the trailer will tend to turn close to the car. You must therefore turn the steering wheel only slightly.

On the Road

Like any driver on the road, you must follow the five keys to safe driving (Smith System) when driving an RV:

1. Aim high in steering.
2. Get the big picture.
3. Keep your eyes moving.
4. Leave yourself an out.
5. Make sure they see you.

In addition, when you drive an RV you always have to think of the length, the width and (what I often forgot) the height. In the case of a motorhome, a good trick I just learned is to install on the front bumper a flexible antenna as high as the highest part of the vehicle. When you drive under an over-hanging structure, there will be no need to get out and check the clearance. Just drive slowly. If you see the antenna move, just back up.

When you are driving, remember to leave room between you and the vehicle in front, enough for a semi-truck or bus that may wish to pass you. Make it easy for those drivers to pull ahead of you; they are not on holidays. Most of them are very helpful to RVers. When you overtake them on an expressway, they usually flash their lights to let you know it is safe to pull over into their lane. (We could help the car drivers the same way). When I have had trouble with my vehicle, truckers are often the only ones who have stopped to help, besides other RVers.

When you are driving a motorhome or pulling a trailer, as a semi-truck passes, you feel drawn to it; you must remain calm and maintain a straight path. When pulling a trailer this suction can cause the trailer to sway; go a bit faster and use the trailer hand brake until everything gets back to normal. If you slam on the brakes or steer roughly, the situation will get worse. The smaller the trailer, the more it will sway.

If you are driving down a highway in the right lane, and see a car merging from the right, first make sure there is nobody on your left, then move over to let the car in. It's a nice gesture and safe driving practice. The same thing applies when a car has stopped on the shoulder of the road. Your safety is at stake. This driver might not see you, and start to enter the roadway.

If you prefer driving 45 mph on a two-lane road, look into your rear view mirror regularly; somebody in a hurry to go to work might want to pass you! As soon as you can, let him go by, as well as any other cars that are in more of a hurry than you.

Never, never drive on the left lane of the road unless you are passing somebody. Remember that no one likes to drive behind an RV that blocks the view . . . it's worse if you block the road! As drivers swear at you, they will have plenty of time to read your license plate and judge badly all people coming from your state or province, as well as all RVers.

Never forget that you cannot stop as fast with an RV as with a car; it is the extra length as well as the weight. Stay far enough behind other cars and try to be even more alert than when driving a car.

If you've been driving a car for years without ever having an accident, you probably think you know all the tricks in the book. You really should read the leaflet published by the Motor Vehicle Bureau; you can get it where you register your car or RV. Read it completely; you'll probably learn a thing or two. Even the guides for bicycles and motorcycles should be enlightening; you'll know more about how drivers will handle their bikes. Better yet, take the six hour 55 Alive driving course sponsored by AARP.

Parking

When you are ready to park in a campground, first, get out of your vehicle and examine the area. Find out where the electrical, water and sewer outlets are. Discuss with your partner the items that must be avoided, like cut-off roots that could puncture a tire, a branch that is too low, etc., and agree upon which way to go and where to stop.

One of the favorite pastimes of campers sipping a refreshing drink while taking it easy is watching newcomers who argue while parking their RVs. I used to suggest to my husband, who prefered to do most of the driving, to park off the road, out of the way, and rest for a while before parking for good. It is best to keep silent for this operation and use signs that you have practiced beforehand. For those who prefer speaking, it's better to use walkie-talkies than to yell back and forth when you are tired and cannot hear above the noise of the engine. The one that helps the driver to back up should be behind the vehicle, and should be visible in the rear view mirror. The job of the helper is to indicate to which side the back end of the RV should go (not to which side the steering wheel should turn).

Departure Checklist

A Checklist for the Outside

1. You already know what you should do about your car when preparing for a trip. Do the same checks for your towing vehicle, your motorhome or/and your towed car. You should make sure you have all the spare parts and the tools that could be useful.
2. Check the trailer hitch for tightness at points where it connects to vehicle and ball to hitch.
3. Check trailer tires.
4. Check trailer brake lights, turn signal and interior lights.
5. Check the trailer/auxiliary battery level and terminals.
6. Check the RV air vents for blockage.
7. Check the water pump.
8. Fill up the water tank.

 9. Check the level in the LP tanks.
10. Empty holding tanks.
11. Disconnect electrical, TV and telephone hookups.
12. Roll up the awning.
13. See that all exterior doors are closed.
14. Remove wheel chocks.
15. Raise jacks and levelers.

A Checklist for the Inside

16. Shut off appliances.
17. Check weight distribution.
18. Close doors, cupboards.
19. Check fire extinguisher.
20. Check smoke detector.
21. Secure loose items.
22. Add holding tank chemical.
23. Roll down TV antenna.
24. Close interior doors.
25. Secure the TV.
26. Lock the refrigerator door.
27. Switch the refrigerator to LP.
28. Close all the windows and air vents.

Before getting in your vehicle, be sure the TV antenna is down; walk around the RV. Did you leave some pliers in front? Is there a cat asleep in front of a wheel? Should you drive out of the area at a different angle? Are there any obstacles? Is the door locked? Is the step up?

When you stop to gas up, turn off the pilot light of the stove and the refrigerator before hand, for safety's sake. While you're stopped, check your tires. Is the awning safely secured? Check the trailer hitch.

People say they hate to pull a trailer and they would be afraid of driving a motorhome. But modern RVs are equipped with safe hitches and are easier to handle than they used to be. They are just a longer, wider and higher car; after a little practice, you may like driving them better than your little car. They might not respond as fast in the traffic but they sure feel safer. So, fasten your seat-belt and have a good trip!

RV Maintenance

You need to examine the roof of your RV every few months. Use a board to walk and kneel down on so you do not put too much weight between the beams (for a trailer). About once a year, apply the same kind of putty used by the manufacturer along the joints and around vents. Do an especially neat job around the TV antenna, so that you do not have trouble raising it. Give a good coat of wax to the exterior once in a while, especially if you intend to spend some time near the ocean, where salt in the air causes corrosion.

As for mechanical maintenance, it's the same as for your car. Send for the guides listed under RV Information in the Appendix. In following their instructions, you will adopt a maintenance routine that will prevent many problems and expenses. And it will keep your RV like new.

When you need major repairs, and you're away from your dealer, it's best to go to another dealer of the same brand or go to chains like U-Haul, Camping World, Sears, Firestone, Mr. Muffler, K-Mart, etc. Always ask for an estimate. Most Goodyear shops will give you a warranty. Check the time for the repair and get the mechanic to personally sign the bill you're paying. Keep the receipt; if something has not been fixed properly, you can stop at another member of the same chain, and maybe they'll remedy the problem for free.

If you are like most readers, you have a house or two and perhaps two cars to maintain, so that there is always something going wrong somewhere, which costs money and much of your valuable time. Try to remember the frustration of that state of affairs when, soon I hope, you are free, traveling in your RV, with no other unit (no house, I hope) to maintain. If then, something goes wrong with your RV, don't get angry, be happy!

CHAPTER 15

How Do You Deal with Nature's Surprises?

Fire

Have you ever thought about what you would do if you had a fire and you were inside your RV? Of course, your first reaction should be to get out! This is what my friend Dick Maser, retired fire captain, himself an RVer, tells me to do. If you cannot reach a door, be sure you know which window is the fire escape. Do you know how to open it?

There are musts, as far as security is concerned. First of all, install a smoke detector far enough from your stove and about six inches from the ceiling. You can add a hatch opening in the roof large enough so a person can get out; some RV dealers will install it. If there is no fire escape in the back of your RV, keep a baseball bat or an axe in this section so you can break a window and escape. Do not attempt to gather up papers or money. Remember that an RV burns very rapidly. If you are trapped, stay close to the floor where there is more air, and crawl towards the exit. If your clothes catch on fire, lie down and roll over to put out the flames. But the best precaution is prevention. Always keep your equipment such as the stove and the furnace in good operating order so they do not become fire hazards. Work out an evacuation plan with other passengers. Get adequate insurance coverage, so if a fire should break out, you will think only to save your life!

Buy a bigger fire extinguisher, know how to use it and have it checked periodically. Check your propane gas lines regularly for leaks. Better still, install a gas leak detector. Shut off all pilots when you gas up or fill your propane tank. Carry propane or gasoline in legal containers. Store them upright in a well ventilated section. In a campground, connect your hose with a Y so you can install a second hose long enough to reach around your RV, in case of fire.

Wind, Sand and Hail Storms

Wind storms and the frequent sand storms of the desert regions hit without warning. If you see such a storm coming while you are on the road, slow down and put on your lights and flashers. These storms can affect your visibility; if you hit the car in front of you, you can start a chain reaction. If possible get off the road; park your RV facing the wind, situate yourself comfortably and shut off the lights. This storm could last a few minutes or long hours. If you cannot get off the road, park your RV as far to the right as possible, shut off the motor and the lights and put on your emergency brakes.

If you are in a campground and you hear a storm warning on the radio, roll up your awning, bring in your chairs, garbage cans, etc. For hail storms, take the same precautions; but there is nothing you can do to prevent damage to your

RV by the hail. Make sure your insurance covers such damage.

Tornadoes

Of all the storms that sweep the earth, tornadoes are the most violent. They take the form of a black funnel, and they are as noisy as a freight train. You can hear them from a distance of twenty-five miles. When the sky darkens, it is wise to listen to a radio or watch TV. If mention is made of a tornado watch, it means that there could be one in the making. Sometimes, there is not even a cloud in the sky. If "a tornado is heading towards" the area where you are; take cover immediately. A tornado warning means one has been sighted, and you must take cover, just in case. The pathway of a tornado is very narrow and many do not even touch down, but why take a chance? Get out of your RV, find some protection from flying objects in a building, far away from the windows, in a hallway or under a staircase.

If you are on the road and you see a tornado, park your RV, if possible, under an underpass, get out and lie down on the ground. Do not remain in a depressed area, as tornadoes are often followed by heavy rainfalls that flood everything. When it is over use channel 9 on your CB and tell the police where the tornado has hit.

Sudden Floods

As mentioned above, severe winds and rain storms will flood ravines, canyons, rivers and dried beds. You must think about this possibility when you park your RV. If flooding should start where you are, and you cannot drive away, get out and find higher ground. Better to risk losing your RV than risk losing your life!

Hurricanes

Hurricanes are usually preceded by considerable advance warnings. Being mobile, you have ample time to get you and your RV out of the way. If you happen to be in a region known as an hurricane area during the season, you should be alert to the weather forecasts, and keep your vehicle in repair and your tanks ready to go. If you have to evacuate the area, follow the route recommended on the radio. If you happen to cross an area after a hurricane has passed through, beware of fallen electrical wires and other objects on the road. Remember that when the center of the eye of the hurricane passes, wind calms down, but comes back violently from the opposite direction.

Snow Storms

Normally, nomads are far away from snow, but sometimes they travel north. If a severe snow storm is predicted, it is usually accompanied by winds to forty-five mph and an temperature of 10°F or less. If glazed frost or drizzle is expected, the roads will be very slippery. When you hear such predictions, get off the road and take cover in a protected area where you can stay for a while without fear of being snowed in so that you will not be able to get out after the snow is over. Do not expect to stop in a campground as most are closed in the winter. If you must drive during a snow storm, be aware of your visibility and lack of traction; install winter windshield wipers, use antifreeze windshield cleaner and equip your RV with good winter tires. It is recommended that you carry a pressurized can of de-icer for the windshield, the wipers and the locks.

Drive with your lights on at all times, and signal your turns well in advance. Brake very carefully to prevent skidding. If need be, pump your brakes and come to a stop gradually. If you have a CB, leave it on the trucker's channel

(19 in the U.S.A., 10 or 12 in Canada). You will hear information on road conditions. Watch for black ice, a thin layer of invisible ice. Take care when you see other vehicles skidding without apparent reason or stopped sideways along the road and sand barrels on the side; all these indicate a slippery area. Bridges could also be slippery. Slow down but do not stop unless your RV is skidding or is not following a straight line.

When you leave the road, look for firm ground. The berm or shoulder of a road may look firm but is often frozen and will become muddy when the sun comes out. Always park your RV in the direction you wish to take when you leave.

Do not forget that snow storms may last many days. Be careful not to use too much power from your battery. If you think the battery could freeze (especially if it's old), wrap it with an old cloth or some newspapers. Water lines in your cooking area may freeze if you do not leave the cupboard doors open. When you are using your stove or your furnace, do not forget to open a window just in case there is a gas leak you are not aware of.

Earthquakes

If you are in your RV during an earthquake, stay calm; you are in the safest place, as RVs are built to resist shaking! However, it could be shaken to the point where propane gas lines could be damaged; check carefully. If you are away from your RV, do not stand underneath electric wires, near posts or building ledges which could fall on you. When you take to the road again, watch for holes, muddy areas, cracked pavements or other obstructions.

Thunder Storms

Do not park under a tree during a severe storm as lightning can hit and cause the tree to fall on your RV. Otherwise, remain calm as your RV is as safe as a car, with rubber tires which prevent grounding. There is a special radio for getting twenty-four hour reports on weather, wherever you are. Ask your RV dealer or any RV accessories store for.

In the U.S.A. you can call at no charge 1-800-323-4180 to get a weather report, road conditions and a list of free or low cost attractions in the region the call comes from. Similar services are also available in many rest areas.

During the eight years I have been traveling fulltime, I have experienced only one hail storm in Oklahoma City strong enough to damage the aluminium siding on one side of our motorhome.

It doesn't matter whether you are on the road as a nomad or not. Catastrophies and storms can happen anywhere and you cannot control that. All you can do is learn to protect yourselves the best way possible.

CHAPTER 16

How Do You Prepare for the Life of a Free Spirit

The manner in which you decide to change your lifestyle and the way you go about it will affect the way you feel about it later. First, gather as much information as possible by reading this book and others like it, by referring to the sources provided in the Appendix and by talking to RVers. If you think that the nomad life would suit you but you have never traveled in an RV, rent one. Once you are in this home on wheels, imagine what it would be like if you had everything you need with you, as you do at home. Remember . . . you would have all the time in the world if you were a nomad! Renting an RV is quite expensive, but it's money well spent if it helps you to make the right decision. It will also give you a better idea of which RV type would best suit your nomadic life.

To Sell or Not to Sell Your House

There are pros and cons to whether or not you should sell your house. Should you decide to keep your home, ask yourself if it is the kind of house you will need when you retire. You may be attached to it because it's where you raised your family, but it may be too big for your needs or it's getting old and will need lots of repairs once you stop traveling. You can sell the house now; and later on, you can rent or buy a house that will be better suited to your needs at that time.

If you're quite young, it might be wiser to keep your house as an investment (who knows?). If you are near retirement age, maybe you don't have to be preoccupied with making or not making a profit later. If you sell your house, you won't have to worry about leaving it empty; and you no longer have all your eggs in the same basket. You can save the money you would have to spend on maintenance, heating, insurance and taxes.

Besides, the money will not be tied up anymore and should you invest the proceeds of the sale (a substantial amount with today's market prices), it will yield a sizeable income. When you add this to the money you are saving from the expenses you will not have any more (minus income tax), it will leave you with a nice source of income. Figure it out, put it down on paper, compare. And unless you invest your money for many years at a time, it will be more easily accessible than in a house. It can come in handy.

Renting Out Your House

If you leave your house vacant, it can be vandalized or burglarized. If you rent it, you get some revenue and you still have a house for when you need it. But, unless you're very lucky (I'm an ex real estate agent and I know how it works), you're taking a chance that your house might not be well kept, even be damaged. Maintenance and repairs will cost more, especially if you are not there to supervise. If the tenants don't pay the rent, it will be difficult to evict them (discuss that with a lawyer).

Psychological Aspects

If you sell your house and all its contents (as I did) and you live all year round in your RV, traveling from one place to another, you become in some people's eyes, a vagabond with money. You now have only money invested and a house without grounds. For me and thousands of nomads, this means freedom. However, for many people, this is psychologically a loss of identity.

If you think you belong to the second group, it will be better to keep your house or at least rent a small apartment where you can store the items that are dear to you. Or, you can buy a summer cottage or a mobile home or just a piece of land where you can park your RV. To own some property may make you feel better through your years of nomadic life.

I, for one, wonder if, psychologically, it is a good thing to leave a house behind when we decide upon the nomadic life. With a house empty or rented in the back of your mind, you are not really free. And, probably, one must always compare between the little house on wheels and the big one with the huge kitchen and loads of cupboards for the odds and ends that can be useful at times.

On the other hand, it might appeal to you to do as my husband and I did in 1981; we sold the houses and everything and put the essentials in a motorhome and left to roam around freely. Forget about a house and the eternal housekeeping! You will take full advantage of all the benefits of this new way of life and minimize its inconveniences. Adaptation is the word.

In every situation, there are two sides of the coin. One must choose. Some people can never choose; they let life decide for them. They remain on the fence, always un-decided, always unsatisfied. For all kind of reasons they choose to be negative instead of positive; they are seldom happy.

Furniture and Treasures

What will you do with your most prized possessions if you haven't kept a house, a cottage or someplace else. Put them in storage? Think of the cost, $100 per month or more, plus transportation, plus depreciation if they are not properly stored in a place where they will be well covered, protected from fire hazards, from pests and from insects. Should you get a modern apartment later on, do you think your furniture will fit? Will you still want it? Your appliances will be many years older!

You can leave your furniture with your children or friends (they might not want it) with the understanding that you will take it back some day and that they can keep it, should you die in the meantime. If you want to get rid of your furniture and your children want it, you can do the same thing as a lady I know. She wrote down the name of each article on a piece of paper. Last Christmas, each child picked the pieces of paper one by one, in turn, until there was none left. Then, they exchanged the items among themselves. This way, she could never be suspected of playing favorites, and every-body was happy, including the lady.

Rosemary had a hard time making up her mind to sell her belongings until the day not long after her neighbor's death when she saw the deceased's children with a salesman from a second-hand furniture shop. He hauled everything away in his truck. "I understood then, that everything that has a sentimental value for me, probably doesn't have any for anybody else and I should not put too much value on mate-rial things. I sold everything and felt really relieved."

What to Keep

When deciding what to keep, think of space; also, remember that the weight of what you're going to carry around should not exceed the capacity of the engine that is pulling the RV. The more weight you pull, the more fuel you consume. You don't want to bring only the absolute minimum (you are not entering a convent), but you also don't want to be stuck with things that you will use only three times a year. You have to be very strict with yourself. As often as possible, choose articles that will have two or three uses. It is preferable to sell your whole wardrobe and buy a few mix and match items with the money; you will pick clothes that harmonize with the color of your (very few now) shoes and accessories in one basic color. From now on, you will want to pay attention to which clothes you wear and wash more often—that will tell you what to keep.

Getting rid of one's possessions (they possess us so) is one of the hardest commitments. I've discussed this with other nomads, and they've told me it was the source of unpleasant controversy with mates. But you can get through it if you keep thinking of the better days that are in store for you—all the free days, months; years ahead.

Going Back Home

Going home, that is back to where you have spent the best years of your life, is an emotional experience for most of us. You can go home without owning a house or any other type of dwelling. Your memories, your sentimental links bring you home in thought and sometimes for a visit. You will park for a day or two in front of your child's or your friend's house. After you make the rounds, you keep traveling or you may choose to stay around for a few weeks and rent a space in a nearby campground where your grandchildren come to see you and use the swimming pool.

And, one day, you might want to stop traveling and settle down again, back home. Owning nothing, you will be free to choose what will be best suited to you at that time. You will probably want to live in a residence for retired people with all the activities that will keep you busy. You will be able to sign a lease, free as a bird, without having to wait for the sale of your house, of your unsuitable furniture and all the "stuff" you've been accumulating through all those years. You will settle down with brand new furniture and feel like a newly-wed. Another adaptation, another adventure! And you'll still use your RV for rallies or short trips, so you can again be in the country, enjoying again "life in a house on wheels."

Financial Inventory

Before deciding to live like a nomad two months or two years down the line, you must determine exactly what your financial situation is. How much do you get per month if you are already retired? How much would you get if you stopped working next week? Draw up a list of your sources of income, including pension and social security, army or government allowances, income from real estate you intend to keep, stocks and bonds, interest on the proceeds of the sale of your house, money owed to you, etc.

Think of all the expenses that will stay the same: personal insurance, tuition fees for one of your children, etc. Looking at this, you can almost decide your departure date! At least now you know your probable net income. By the time you finish reading this book, you will know how much it will cost you to live as a nomad. If you find out you don't have enough, ask yourself how long you want to wait before starting this life and how you are going to go about getting more money. Establish your working plan, right now!

Official Residence for a Fulltimer

Do you know that you can choose your place of residence (now that you have no permanent one), according to what's best for you now? You can choose the state where there is no income tax, where you can renew your RV registration by mail and where there are all kinds of good benefits. Your residence could be where you get your mail, the address of your mail forwarding service. The booklet "Selecting an RV Home Base" will help you decide. Another one, "What to Do about Your Money when You Move to Florida" gives advice that applies to fulltime RVers. It recommends that you move all "property" with you when you move from one state to another to avoid double taxation. After you read these books and you decide where you want to establish residence, it's advisable to consult a lawyer who has experience in probate in that state and have him draw up new wills.

Your Will and Other Matters

As you are making your financial inventory, why not make a list of your assets and decide today who will inherit what, if you should die tomorrow. Even if you sell everything, you still own your RV, your investments, your insurance. Do you have a will? Is it current with your present situation? You can make a will now and amend it when you become a nomad; it does not cost very much and you will have peace of mind. Your attorney can help you. Don't put off until tomorrow such an important decision. Send for the free "Will" booklet.

I mentioned earlier the importance of credit cards. Before you retire is the best time to apply for them; ask for a much higher limit than your present one. If you are already retired, apply now for them, with the highest limit you can get.

At your bank and other financial institutions, get information about the latest electronic systems to pay your bills, withdraw money from your bank account or any other service that can help a traveler. (see Chapter 6.) Are your pension checks and other regular income deposited directly into your account? Whether you become a nomad or not, you should avail yourself of this service. You could be suddenly hospitalized or decide to go on a trip and you would not have to worry about your checks being left in the mail box.

Is your house insured adequately, that is, for its present market value? It might be worth many thousands more than what you paid for it just a few years back . . . If you leave your house vacant, should your house be visited regularly? Discuss this with your insurance broker. Check also your group medical insurance and/or get complete coverage for hospital and medical expenses in case you become sick outside your province, your state or your country. Your insurance broker, a travel agency and Blue Cross can provide this insurance. Your car and your RV should be properly insured. To be on the safe side, your broker should note that your RV is used year round as a home.

Club group policies are especially favorable to RVers. (see Chapter 12) Very often, you will have to show a proof of identity. The best ones are your driver's license or your citizenship cards if they bear your picture. This is the time to apply for an official card with your photo.

Now is the time for every man to make sure the woman in his life can drive the car and the RV. She should know how to operate all the RV systems, so in the event of illness, she can take over. And every man should learn how to manage in the kitchen, do the laundry and the housekeeping. One of the many advantages in being two is that one can replace the other should an emergency arise; it is a security for both partners. In the meantime, the two mates share the cooking and housekeeping, and have more time to share the agreeable undertakings. Now is also the time to take courses in first aid, CPR, basic mechanics, foreign language, anything that can help you on the road or anywhere else.

If you died tomorrow, would your heirs know where to find your will, your bank accounts, your investments, your insurance policies, your credit cards, what is owed to you, what you owe and what you own? Probably not. Have you given a thought to the problems they'll have? The best thing to do is leave all the information in an envelope to be opened in case of death or total disability. Enclosed would be the name of the attorney who has your will, a letter stating what kind of funeral arrangements you want, the organs you wish to donate, what you want done with your personal belongings; in short, everything that must be known immediately and is not included in the will. Also, in the envelope should be a list with details about your place of birth, your social security number, date of your divorce, addresses of your children, any data that your survivors might not be sure of and might need to know at that time. Don't forget to include a list of your insurance policies, the names of brokers, your pensions, your investments, your bank accounts, your credit cards, your debts and the money owed to you.

Make a copy for yourself, one for your partner and at least one other person. I wonder how many wills have never been carried out, how many insurance policies have never been paid out, how many bank accounts have never been found because the heirs never knew they existed.

Just Before Leaving

Before you leave, you should have a written evaluation of your health from your doctor and your dentist. Your broker and your bank manager should have your forwarding address, your insurance policies should be paid in advance, your will should be updated. In addition be sure your safety box is paid for, (I carry a fireproof safety box so I have any document I might need on the road. Each of my kids have an envelope like I described) your driver's license and registration are paid up, your passport is in order (you might decide to pop over to Mexico), and everybody knows your forward-ing address and your phone service number. You filed a change of address card at the post office. (see Chapter 8)

After your family and friends have been kissed goodbye, dry your tears. In a few miles, you will start to relax and in a few more miles, you will start to feel free, and in a few more days you will pinch yourself, wondering if your new life is real. In a few weeks you'll wonder why you did not start before. Enjoy it! Don't be sad if you have sold your house; you probably won't want it after living in a carefree house on wheels. You might even want to settle down somewhere else! There are some retirement villages where you can buy a beautiful house with a special garage for both your car and your RV. There are mountain cabins also that are set up that way.

CHAPTER 17

Conclusion

Now that you know what this lifestyle is all about, do you want to live like this? You are decided? Good for you! I hope you hit the road soon, and let me know of your experiences, OK? Perhaps you will be in a position to give me tips for my next book.

I know that not everyone is resolute. I can imagine some readers saying: "I would like to live fulltime in an RV, but. . . ."

. . . but I still have a son at the university."

—Did you ever figure out how much it costs you to keep a house for your children's convenience? If you were able to sell it, the interest on the sale price would pay the rent of an apartment for your son; it would teach him to manage on his own, which he will have to do sooner or later, and the sooner the better, according to psychologists. And, you would be free. For you, for all parents, "the sooner the better" is even more true; who knows what will happen to us as we get older?

For those "But I don't have the ideal RV and can't spare buying another one" people:

—Leave anyway. It's better to start like this and discover exactly what you will need when you are ready to buy later.

For those "but I have often been sick lately" people:

—Maybe a change in your lifestyle will do you much good; try it! It seems that many of our health problems are psychological. Loneliness and the fear of growing old are often the cause of an illness.

For those "but my husband and I can't stand each other" people:

—In a new environment, doing new things together, you might look at each other differently. This might be what your marriage needs. Try this life! What have you got to lose?

For those "but I have an aging mother whom I do not dare leave" people:

—Is there someone else who can take care of her while you are away? If there is, write to your mother often and phone her regularly. Perhaps, hearing of your experiences may smooth down her loneliness much better than regular visits when you have nothing new to discuss. Or, take her with you! I have met an eighty-eighty-year-old lady who was quite happy to travel in a motorhome with her daughter and her son-in-law. (Between us, she had more pep than he.) She had been to the hairdresser in the afternoon and at the grocery. Yet at our place (our RV, of course) that evening she would have kept sipping wine and talking long after her son-in-law was hinting about going home (to his RV, of course). She was describing to me all the advantages of "camping" instead of traveling by car and using motels.

For those "but I am too young; I am supposed to have a permanent job at my age" people!

—Because others think that way, because society is built that way, you are not obliged to stay in that mold. It is your life. You have the right to live it the way you want.

For those "but I could not live far from my grandchildren" people:

—Imagine that their parents find a better job, far away; it might happen and they might leave. Why not live new experiences, make new friends, be busy living your own exciting life and be less concerned with your grandchildren over which you have no control anyway; this is your children's job, and you probably are not too happy with the way they do it anyway. Each generation has its own way and you're not supposed to interfere and if you stay around you will get frustrated.

For the "but I can't let go all of my treasures" people:

—Loan them, store them; you will see, after a while on the road, that their value has greatly diminished in your eyes. Just remember that there are not many of these possessions you can bring into a senior citizens' home. While you have an interesting mobile life is the right time to get used to a less encumbered living.

For those "but I will be lost without my garden and my workshop" people:

—You will have so many new things to do; why continue to do what you have done all your life? Anyway, you can always pull a small trailer to carry your shop; others do it.

For those "but I lack mechanical knowledge to take care of my RV" people:

—No way can you be worse than I am! I am careful to follow the maintenance schedule and get my motorhome to garages and RV service places all over for verifications and/or repairs. But, for you, becoming an apprentice mechanic could be a new hobby: many RVers will be glad to give you a hand.

For all the "but maybe I should wait; in five years, I will be entitled to a better pension and I will feel more secure" people:

—You might also feel nothing if you are not in this world

anymore. Pardon me, for being blunt, but we should all remember that we will not live forever. Being secure is really being confident that we can manage. Looking back, most of us have managed in bad situations that will never happen again, so let's be happy while we are alive and stop worrying.

For those "but I am afraid of leaving an environment I know so well" people:

—It's normal. Familiar things make us feel more secure. A baby is afraid to walk; it's a strange experience for him. But, if he walks, he progresses; he is happy to have overcome his fear. This is life.

You need only three things to start a beautiful new life: a little money, a recreational vehicle and the will to start. Even if this book shows you how to do it, even if it gives you the incentive to do it, there is only one person capable of doing it: YOU. Get yourself an RV, arrange for your mail and access to your money and go! You don't need all kinds of planning. Just go! Take to the road, stop when you feel like it, but go! Don't wait for later; later might never come! GO!

For commentaries and suggestions, you can write to me so I can share them in my next book. Thank you.

Happy life on wheels!

Rollanda D. Masse
FMCA member #41126,
P.O. Box 44209
Cincinnatti, OH 45244

Appendix

Camping/RV Clubs

GOOD SAM
29901R Agoura Rd.
Agoura, CA 91301
Phone: 800-234-3450
CA800-382-3455

FAMILY MOTOR COACH ASSOC.
(FMCA)
8291 Clough Pike
P.O. Box 3393R
Cincinnatti, OH 45244
Phone: 800-543-3622

ESCAPEES INC.
(SKPs)
Box 310R
Livingston, TX 77351
Phone: (409) 327-8873

FRIENDLY ROAMERS
P.O. Box 3393R
North Shore, CA 92254-0968
Phone: (619) 393-3021

NATIONAL CAMPERS & HIKERS
  ASSOC.
(NCHA)
4804R Transit Rd.
Depew, NY 14043
Phone: (716) 668-6242

For Handicapped RVers

HANDICAPPED TRAVEL CLUB
667 "J" Ave.
Coronado, CA 91118
Phone: (619) 435-5213
also at:
Rt 1 Box 77
Lewis, KS 67552

ACHIEVERS INTERNATIONAL
(FMCA Chapter)
9251 East Lake
Otisville, MI 48463
Phone: (517) 871-4377

For Singles

LONERS ON WHEELS
(LOWs)
808R Lester St.
Poplar Bluff, MO 63901
Phone: (817) 626-4538

WHAT I NEED
(WIN)
P.O. Box 2010R
Sparks, NV 89432-1010

SINGLES INTERNATIONAL
(FMCA Chapter)
P.O. Box 1066R
Kearny, AZ 85237

Special Interest
AMATEUR RADIO
(FMCA Chapter)
1380 Evergreen Ave. N.E.
Salem, OR 97301
Phone: (503) 362-2859

FULLTIMERS
(FMCA Chapter)
P.O. Box 44209R
Cincinnatti, OH 45244

MOBILE MISSIONARY
    ASSISTANCE PROGRAM
(MMAP)
1736 N. Sierra Bonita Ave.
Pasadena, CA 91104
Phone: (818) 791-8663

SPECIAL MILITARY ACTIVE
    RETIREES TRAVEL
(SMART)
P.O. Box 730
Fallbrook, CA 92028

RV BIRD WATCHERS
409 Washington Ave.

Loogootee, IN 47553
Phone: (812) 295-2729

TRAVELING RETIRED
    AMERICAN VOLUNTEERS
(TRAV)
P.O. Box 5645
Hollywood, FL 33083-5645

Camping Places

Commercial—Rent Only

INDIAN CREEK PARK
17340R San Carlos Blvd.
Ft. Myers Beach, FL 33931-3098
Phone: (813) 466-6060

GOLDEN VILLAGE
37250R Florida Ave. W.
Hamet, CA 92343
Phone: (714) 925-2518

VOYAGER RV RESORT
8701R South Kolb Rd.
Tucson, AZ 85706
Phone: (602) 746-2000

TROPIC STAR
1401R South Cage,
Pharr, TX 78577
Phone: (512) 787-5957

KOA CAMPGROUND CHAIN
P.O. Box 30558R
Billings, MT 59114
Phone: (406) 248-7444

KOA MONTREAL SOUTH
130R Monette St.
St. Philippe de Laprairie,
Quebec, Canada JOL 2KO
Phone: (514) 659-8626

Condominium

OUTDOOR RESORTS OF
  AMERICA (Chain)
(ORA)
2400R Crestmoor Rd.
Nashville TN 37215
Phone: (615) 244-5237

BLUEWATER KEY
P.O. Box 409R
Lower Sugar Loaf Key, FL 33044
Phone: 800-237-2266

THE GREAT OUTDOORS
(Championship golf resort)
4505R Cheney Hwy. (SR-50)
Titusville, FL 32783-5667
Phone: 800-621-2267

For Members Only

CAMPER RANCH CLUB OF
  AMERICA
P.O. Box 328R
Conroe, TX 77305
Phone: (409) 756-3328

ESCAPEE CLUB CO-OP
  CAMPGROUNDS & RETREATS
Box 310R
Livingston, TX 77351
Phone: (409) 327-8873

Chains of Membership
Campgrounds

CAMP COAST TO COAST
1000 16th St. N.W. #840R
Washington, DC 20036
Phone: 800-368-5721
        202-293-8000

RESORT PARKS

INTERNATIONAL
P.O. Box 7738R
Long Beach, CA 90807
Phone: 800-456-7774

THOUSAND TRAILS
15375R 30th Place SE
Bellevue, WA 98001
Phone: (206) 455-3155

(for reservation of above chains)

RESERVATION CLUB
P.O. Box 883R
Live Oak, FL 32060
Phone: 800-843-4039
FL 800-843-7082

(for resales of above chains)

MONROE RESORT RESALES
117 W. 14th Ave. Box 2169R
Gulf Shores, AL 36542

Special Interest

WILLMETTAN NUDIST CAMP
c/o Nudist Parks Guide Assoc.
1703 N. Main St. #E
Kissimee, FL 32743

CLERBROOK RV RESORT
& GOLF
Route 2, Box 107R
Clermont, FL 32711
Phone: 800-346-2307

FOUNTAIN OF YOUTH
SPA & RV PARK
HC#01, Box 12R, Dept. M
Miland, CA 92257
Phone: (619) 348-1340

HORSEWORLD OF SCOTTSDALE
16602R North Pima Rd.
Scottsdale, AZ 85260
Phone: 800-877-8888

ARMED FORCES CAMP GUIDE
2800 Eastern Blvd.
Baltimore, MD 21220

MILITARY RV CAMPING AREAS
P.O. Box 2347R
Falls Church, VA 22042
Phone: (703) 237-0203

Campground Directories
TRAILER LIFE
CAMPGROUNDS & RV SERVICES
29901R Agoura Rd.
Agoura, CA 91301
Phone: 800-234-3450
CA: 800-382-3455

WOODALL'S
CAMPGROUND DIRECTORY
28167R N. Keith Dr.
Lake Forest, IL 60045
Phone: 800-323-9076
IL (708) 362-6700

WHEELERS
CAMPGROUND GUIDE
1310R Jarvis Ave.
Elk Grove Village, IL 60007
Phone: 800-323-8899

KOA CAMPGROUND GUIDE
(chain)
P.O. Box 30558R
Billings, MT 51994
Phone: 406-248-7444

Government Parks
NATIONAL PARKS SERVICE
U.S. DEPT. OF INTERIOR
P.O. Box 37127,
Washington, DC 20013-7127

U.S. FOREST SERVICE
DEPT. OF AGRICULTURE
P.O. Box 2417

Washington, DC 20013
Phone: 800-283-2267

FISH & WILDLIFE REFUGES
DEPT. OF INTERIOR
Washington, DC 20240

BLM PUBLIC AFFAIRS
1800 "C" St, N.W.
Washington, DC 20240

U.S. ARMY COE PUBLIC
    AFFAIRS
20 Massachusetts Ave. N.W.
Washington, DC 20314

FEDERAL ENERGY
    REGULATORY COMMISSION
825 N. Capitol St. N.E.
Washington, DC 20426

OHIO POWER CO.
P.O. Box 328,
MeConnelsville, OH 43756

CANADA'S NATIONAL PARKS
& HISTORIC SITES
ENVIRONMENT CANADA
Hull, Que., Canada K1A OH3
Phone: (819) 997-2800

CAMPING IN THE NATIONAL
    PARK SYSTEMS
U.S. Government Printing Office,
Superintendent of Documents,
Washington, DC 20402

Special Interests, Hobbies
UNCOMMON AND
    UNHERALDED MUSEUMS
Hippocrene Books Inc.
171 Madison Ave.
New York, NY 10016
Phone (212) 685-4371

THE NATIONAL CAVES ASSOC.
DIRECTORY
Box 106,
McMinnville, TN 37110

THE NATIONAL
SPELEOLOGICAL SOCIETY
Cave Avenue,
Huntsville, AL 35810
Phone: (205) 852-1300

ELDERHOSTEL
80 Boylston St Suite 400R
Boston MA 02116

Help for Boondocking

Free Camping

GUIDE TO FREE CAMPGOUNDS
Cottage Publications
24396R Pleasant View Dr.
Elkhart, IN 46517

ESCAPEES CLUB'S CO-OPS
Free areas for club members

FMCA CLUB'S LIST
Spaces at member's for members

Lists of Free Dumping Stations

APCO
1856 Lilac Creek,
Carlsbad, CA 92008

UNOCAL CUSTOMER SERVICE
Box 7600,
Los Angeles, CA 90051

LOW'S CLUB'S LIST
for members

FMCA CLUB'S LIST
FOR MEMBERS

Low Fee Dumping Stations

U-HAUL
LP GAS & RV DUMP STATION
DIRECTORY
Phone: 800-GO-U-HAUL

Mail & Message Services

(For Club Members)

FMCA CLUB

GOOD SAM CLUB

ESCAPEES CLUB

For Anyone Including Non-RVers

MCCA
P.O. Box 2870R
Estes Park, CO 80517
Phone: 800-525-5304

NATO
P.O. Box 1418R
Sarasota, FL 33578
Phone: 800-237-NATO
FL 800-222-NATO

TOMA
P.O. Box 2010R
Sparks, NV 89432

Telephone Information

AT&T TELEMARKETING
P.O. Box 58,
Kansas City, MO 64141
Phone: 800-225-5288

AMERICAN TEL-A-CALL
P.O. Box 27087-E
Tempe, AZ 85282

TELEPHONE USERS ASS.
P.O. Box 2387
Arlington, VA 22202
Phone: (202) 628-5696

Problems

Medical

VIAL OF LIFE CORPORATION
P.O. Box 151150R
Cape Coral, FL 33915
Phone: (813) 458-4422

MEDIC ALERT FOUNDATION
P.O. Box 1009 R
Turloxk, CA 95381-1009
Phone: 800-344-3226

AMERICAN RED CROSS
17th & D St.,
Washington, DC 20006
Phone: (202) 737-8300

AARP PHARMACY MAIL
    SERVICE
510 King St., Dept NBA
Alexandria, VA 22313

AMERICA'S PHARMACY BY
    MAIL
2109 McKinley Ave.
Des Moines, IA 50321
Phone: (515) 287-6872

HILL-BURTON FREE HOSPITAL
    CARE
Phone: 800-638-0742
MD: 800-492-0359

HEALTH CARE ABROAD
923 Investment Bldg
1511 "K" St. N.W.
Washington, DC 20005
Phone: 800-336-3310

ENGLISH SPEAKING DOCTORS
    ALL OVER THE WORLD
(IAMAT)
350 Fifth Ave. #5620
New York, NY 10001

MEDICAL TRAVEL INSURANCE
(for Americans in Canada &
    Canadians out of Canada)
NOMAD INSURANCE
John Ingle & Associates,
710R Bay St.
Toronto, Ont., Canada M5G 9Z9
Phone: (416) 597-0666

Legal & Financial

THE LIVING BANK
(organ donors)
P.O. Box 6725
Houston, TX 77265
Phone: 800-528-2971

"YOUR WILL" BOOKLET
c/o The Salvation Army
30840 Hawtorne Blvd.
Rancho Palos Verdes, CA 90274

"WHAT TO DO ABOUT YOUR
    MONEY WHEN MOVING TO
    ANOTHER STATE"
c/o Barnett Bank
Center Gate Office,
P.O. Box 3076
Sarasota, FL 34230-3076

AMERICAN ASSOC. OF RETIRED
    PERSONS
(AARP)
Investments Dept.
1909 "K" St. N.W.
Washington, DC 20049
Phone: (212) 872-4700

"SELECTING A RESIDENCE"
(state tax & registration info.)
c/o Trailer Life
29901 Agoura Rd.
Agoura, CA 91301
Phone: 800-234-3450
CA 800-382-3455

Everyday RV Life Info

HOUSEKEEPING
c/o Arm & Hammer,
P.O. Box 7648
Princeton, NJ 08540

CHURCH DIRECTORY,
American Business Directories
P.O. Box 27347R
Omaha, NE 68127
Phone (402) 593-4600

GOOD SAM RV COOKBOOK,
29901R Agoura Rd.
Agoura, CA 91301
Phone: 800-234-3450
CA 800-382-3455

Recreational Vehicle Information

RV Companies

ALL CATEGORIES OF RVs

FLEETWOOD ENTERPRISES,
INC.
P.O. Box 7638R
Riverside, CA 92523
Phone: 1-800-444-4905

MOTORHOMES ONLY

WINNEBAGO INDUSTRIES
P.O. Box 152R

Forest City, IA 50436
Phone: (515) 582-3535

TRIPLE E CANADA
Box 1230R
Winkler, MAN. Canada R6W 4C4

Super Luxury Coaches

PEAGSUS AUTOHAUS—
1805 FM 1314
Porter, TX 77365
Phone: (713) 354-3288

THE CLOU LINER—
American RV Inc.
4848 W. Cardinal DR.
Beaumont, TX 77705
Phone: 800-231-6449

Folding Down Long Trailers

TRAILMANOR—
P.O. Box 130,
Lake City, TN 37769
Phone: (615) 426-7426

HI-LO TRAILER CO.
145 Elm St.
Butler, OH 44822
Phone: 800-321-6402
OH: (419) 883-3000

Camping Vans

INTERNATIONAL VEHICLES
CORP.
200R Legion St.
Bristol, IN 46507

PACIFIC COAST VAN & RV LTD.
7454 R 6th St.
Burnaby, BC, V3N 489

RVs for Handicapped
TETON INTERNATIONAL
P.O. Box 2349

Mills, WY 82644
Phone: (307) 235-1525

RICON CORPORATION
11684 Tuxford St.
Sun Valley, CA 91352
Phone: (213) 768-5890

CONTEMPORARY COACH
P.O. Box 152
Goshen, IN 46526
Phone: (219) 533-4161

RV Buying Help

RV DEALERS ASSOCIATION
(RVDA) RV SHOWS
3251 Old Lee Highway Suite 500R
Fairfax, VA 22030
Phone: (703) 591-7130

CANADIAN RV DEALERS
ASSOC (CRVDA)—(RV shows)
201-19623R 56th Ave.
Langley, BC Canada V3A 3X7
Phone: (604) 533-4200

TRAILER LIFE RV BUYER GUIDE
29901R Agoura Rd.
Agoura, CA 91301
Phone: 800-234-3450
CA 800-382-3455

WOODALL'S RV BUYER GUIDE
100 Corporate N. #100R
Bannockburn, IL 60015-1253
Phone: (312) 295-7799

CANADIAN RV GUIDE
703 Evans Ave., Suite 306R
Toronto, ONT
Canada M9C 5E9

RV Rental Companies
U-HAUL RENTAL DIVISION
2727R Central N.

Phoenix, AZ 85036
Phone: 800-821-2712

CRUISE AMERICA/CANADA
5959 Blue Lagoon Dr. #250R
Miami, FL 33126
Phone: 800-327-7778
(305) 591-7511
(Canada:) 800-327-7799

GO VACATIONS INC
24701R Frampton Ave.
Harbor City, CA 90710
Phone: 800-387-3998
(Canada)
129R Carlingview Dr.
Rexdale, Ont., Canada M9W 5E7
Phone: 800-387-6869
(416) 674-1880

RV Insurance
GOOD SAM—
FMCA—
CAMPING COAST TO COAST—
(see individual listings)

ALEXANDER & ALEXANDER
(motorhomes, busses)
600 Fisher Bldg.
Detroit, MI 48202
Phone: 800-521-2942
MI: 800-624-7539

CARAVANNER INSURANCE
(travel trailers)
14805 N. 73rd St.
Scottsdale, AZ 85260
Phone: 800-423-4403

FOREMOST INSURANCE
(stationary RVs
and trip insurance)
5800R Foremost Dr.
Grand Rapids, MI 49501

Phone: 800-237-2060
(616) 942-3000

(*Note:* U.S. companies might not
insure Canadian registered RVs.)

Road and Towing Laws

RULES OF THE ROAD
14650 Lee Rd.
Chantilly, VA. 22021

DIGEST OF MOTOR LAWS
American Auto Assoc.
8111 Gatehouse Rd.
Falls Church, VA 22047
Phone: (703) 222-6541

(Check your local licensing bureau
for RV information.)

Renting Your RV

DOLLARS IN YOUR DRIVEWAY
Halo House Publisher
617 Westland Dr.
Greensburg, PA 15601

JENKINS BUSINESS FORMS
Form #1155 (rental contract)
Mascoutah, IL 62258

BATES MANAGEMENT
6000 S. Eastern Ave. Suite 5-C
Las Vegas, NV 89119
Phone: 1-800-732-2283

Towing a Travel Trailer

TOWING TIPS
Draw Tite, Inc.
40500 Van Horn Rd.
Canton, MI 48188

REESE HITCH
(dual dam sway control)

P.O. Box 1706
Elkhart, IN 46515

U-HAUL HITCH AND RV
  SERVICE
(for info list)
Phone: 800-GO-U-HAUL

CHEVY TRAILERING GUIDE (see
GM dealer)

FORD RV AND TRAILER
  TOWING GUIDE
(see Ford dealer)

Towing a Car

REMCO
4138 S. 89th St., Dept. FR
Omaha, NE 68127
Phone: 800-228-2481
NE: (402) 339-3398

TRAILEX
60R Industrial Park Dr.
Canfield, OH 44406-0553
Phone: (216) 533-6814

KAR TOTE
1R Miller Rd.
Pender, NE 68047
Phone: 800-228-9289
(402) 385-3051

TOMMY'S TRAILERS
1828R Latta Rd.
Ada, OK 74820-8610
Phone: (405) 332-7785

Other Auxiliary Transportation

Bicycle Racks

TOTE-N-STOW CORP.
6301R Arthur,
Merrillville, IN 46410
Phone: (219) 980-5481

Folding Bicycles and Mopeds

PED-MO INTERNATIONAL
P.O. Box 784R
Lake Ronkonkoma, NY 11779
Phone: (516) 588-2522

Motorized Tricycle

PLAMER INDUSTRIES
P.O. Box 707 KT
Endicott, NY 13760
Phone: 800-847-1304
NY (607) 754-1954

Quadracycle

LDC CORPORATION
2505 Koyl Ave.
Saskatoon, SAS S7L 5XB
Phone: (306) 244-2503

Boats

POLY TOTE,
Royal International, Inc.
4401R E. Hearn Rd.,
Phoenix, AZ 85032
Phone: (602) 265-2436

PORTA-BOTE
1074R Independence Ave
Mountain View, CA 94043

CAMP-A-FLOAT
101R S. 30th St.
Phoenix, AZ 85034
Phone: (602) 244-9831

Equipment and Accessories
RV-ID ROOF LETTERS
2236R Wesley Ave
Ocean City, NJ

BEST MADE RV SATELLITES
2356R Sarah South

Fresno, CA 93706
Phone: (209) 266-1043

SOLAR ELECTRIC SYSTEMS
Noel & Barbara Kirkby SKP #752
P.O. Box 12455 SR
Scottsdale, AZ 85267
Phone: (602) 443-8520

CAMPING WORLD RV Catalogue
& stores
650R Three Springs Rd.
Bowling Green, KY 42102-9017
Phone: 800-626-5944 (U.S. and
Canada)

PRIVATE EYE RV SECURITY
3100R W. Segerstrom,
Santa Ana, CA 92704
Phone: 800-854-3172
CA: 800-432-7459

**RV Appliances: ice maker, washer/
dryer, dishwasher, trash
compactor, etc.**

RICHLUND SALES
Route 4, Box 18R
Kentwood, LA 70444
Phone: (504) 229-4922

**Rv Maintenance and Repairs
Books**
LIVING ON WHEELS
(for motorhome care)
Tab Books™R
Blue Ridge Summit, PA 17214

RV HOW-TO-GUIDE
Woodall Publishing Co.
100 Corporate N. #100
Bannockburn, IL 60015

RV OWNERS OPERATION &
MAINTENANCE MANUAL

Intertec, Technical Publishing
P.O. Box 12901R
Overland Park, KS 66212

THE GREASELESS GUIDE
John Meir Publications
P.O. Box 613R
Santa Fe, NM 87504
Phone: 800-888-7504

RV REPAIR & MAINTENANCE
TL Enterprises
29901 Agoura Rd.
Agoura, CA 91301-9861

CHEVROLET MOTORHOME
  CHASSIS SERVICE GUIDE and
  RV SERVICE DIRECTORY
Chevrolet Motor Div.
Consumer Relations Dept.
Warren, MI 48090
Phone: (313) 492-5500

RV SERVICE GUIDE
760R Auburn Ave.
Buffalo, NY 14222

U-HAUL RV SERVICE AND
  DIRECTORY
Phone: 800-GO-U-HAUL

GOODYEAR SERVICE
  WARRANTY
Phone: 800-CAR-1999

STORING & USING YOUR RV
  VIDEO
Bunzer Consulting
P.O. Box 38R
Agoura Hills, CA 99301-0038

Rx FOR RV PERFORMANCE AND
  MILEAGE
TL Enterprises
29901R Agoura Rd.
Agoura, CA 91301

Emergency Road Services
GOOD SAM
FMCA
Coast to Coast
(see clubs listings)

SAFE DRIVER MOTOR CLUB
P.O. Box 25099R
Glendale, CA 91301
Phone: 800-272-6669

CB RESCUE
HELP,
242 Cleveland
Wichita, KS 67214
(Canada) Box 942
Sutton Ont. LOE 1RO

Help for Working Nomads
WORKAMPER NEWS
201 Hiram Rd—HCR34
Box 125R
Heber Springs, AR 72543-9757
Phone: (501) 362-2637

HOW TO TURN YOUR IDEAS
  INTO DOLLARS and THE FLEA
  MARKET ENTREPRENEUR
Pilot Books
103R Cooper St.,
Babylon, NY 11702
Phone: (516) 422-2225

SMALL TOWN FESTIVALS &
  FAIRS N/L
Curtis Enterprises
Dept B. P.O. Box 204R
Carson, NV 89702

CLOWNS OF AMERICA
  INTERNATIONAL CLUB (info.
  for amateurs)
1315 Boulevard
New Haven, CT 06511
Phone: (203) 624-0438

NATIONAL ACADEMY RV
TECHNICIAN SCHOOL
14 Foundry St. #104R
Stroudsburg, PA 18360
Phone: (707) 424-5596

LINE DANCE MUSIC
National Association of Swing
Dancers
P.O. Box 9841R
Colorado Springs, CO 80932

LINE DANCE MUSIC
Master Record
P.O. Box 37676R
Phoenix, AZ 85069

THE DONUT MAN
9851 13th Ave. N.
Dept xxx
Minneapolis, MN 55441
Phone: 800-328-8213

BADGE-A-MINIT
Dept. HH389,
348 N. 30th Rd.
Box 800R
Lasalle, IL 61301

WRITER'S DIGEST BOOKS,
1507R Dans Ave.
Cincinnatti, OH 45207

Help for Nomads with Children
AMERICAN SCHOOL (grades 9–
12)
850 E 58th St.
Chicago, IL 60637
Phone: (312) 947-3300

CALVERT SCHOOL (up to 8th
grade)
105 Tuscany Rd.
Baltimore, MD 21210
Phone: (301) 243-6030

INDEPENDENT STUDY (high-
school & university)
University of Nebraska/Lincoln
Room #269,
Lincoln, NE 68583-0900
Phone: (402) 972-1926

PARENTS RIGHTS ON
EDUCATION
12571 Northwinds Dr.
St. Louis, MO 63141
Phone: (314) 434-4171

SCHOOLING AT HOME
John Muir Pulications
P.O. Box 613R
Santa Fe, NM 87504
Phone: 800-888-7504

Help for RVers With Pets
PET SWITCHBOARD
3075 Alhambra Dr. #101
Shingle Springs, CA 95682
Phone: 800-824-7888

CATWATCHING OR
DOGWATCHING
Crown Publishers
225 Park Ave. S
NY, NY 10003
Phone: (212) 254-1600

PET I.D. TAGS
Harry Jones
Rt. 5, Box 310-840
Livingston, TX 77351

Help for Handicapped
INDEPENDENT LIVING (driver
training)
Memorial Hospital
615 N. Michigan St.
South Bend, IN 46601
Phone: (219) 654-8731

MOBILITY INTERNATIONAL
(contacts)
Colombo St.
London, SE1 8DP, England
(see RV information for special
RVs)

To Meet Other Single RVers
TRAVEL COMPANION
EXCHANGE
Box 833R
Amityville, NY 11701

GOLDEN COMPANIONS
Box 754R
Pellman, WA 99163

PARTNERS IN TRAVEL
P.O. Box 491145R
Los Angeles, CA 90049

TRAVEL PARTNERS NETWORK
610R Victoria St.
San Francisco, CA 94127

RETIRED SINGLES
P.O. Box 642R
Yucaipa, CA 92399
Phone: (714) 790-2433

**Villages of Houses with RV
Garages**
VAGABOND TOWNHOME
DUPLEX
Tri-Development Corp.
P.O. Box 247R
Deming, NM 88031

VOYAGERS HOME PORT
Yosemite Vista Estates
22625R Ferretti Rd.
Groveland, CA 95321
Phone: 800-631-6601

CONVERTIBLE MOUNTAIN

HOMESITES, Indian Falls
Cashiers/Sapphire, NC
Phone: 800-446-5310
Florida: (813) 597-3990

ESCAPEES CLUB RETREAT
HOMESITES
Rt. 5, Box 310R
Livingston, TX 77351
Phone: (409) 327-8873

**Organized Tours, Cruises,
Caravans**

GOOD SAM
FMAC
CAMP COAST TO COAST
CAMPING WORLD
CAMP-ORAMA
SANBORN (Mexican car
insurance)
(see individual listings)

TRACKS TO ADVENTURE
2811R Jackson #K,
El Paso, TX 79930
Phone: (915) 565-9627

CARAVANAS VOYAGERS
1155R Larry Mahan #H,
El Paso, TX 79925

POINT SOUTH
8463R Aura Ave.
Northridge, CA 91324
Phone: (818) 701-6944

CREATIVE WORLD RALLIES &
CARAVANS
606R N. Carrolton Ave.
New Orleans, LA 70119
Phone: (504) 486-7259

AMIGO RV TOURS
P.O. Box 43201R

Las Vegas, NV 89116
Phone: (702) 452-8271

INTERNATIONAL CARAVANING
   ASSOC.
Mr. John M. Jeffery,
Nomads Gardens R
Goring Road,
Steyning, W. Sussex,
BN4 3HA England

CHARLES GRIFFITH
2952R South Lincoln St.
Englewood, CO 80110
Phone: (303) 761-9820

NEW ZELAND TOURS
222e Cottonwood Ln.
Casa Grande, AZ 85222
Phone: (602) 836-5755

NEW ZEALAND MOTORHOME
   TOURS
Rd. 11
Hastings, New Zealand

ALASKA CARAVAN
   ADVENTURES
2506R Glenkerry Dr.
Anchorage, AK 99504
Phone: (907) 338-1439

ALASKA YUKON RV CARAVANS
P.O. Box 1896R
Hyder, AK 99923
Phone: 800-426-9865

On Your Own

GYPSYING (ABROAD) AFTER 40,
John Muir Publications
P.O. Box 613R
Santa Fe, NM 87504
Phone: 800-888-7504

EUROPEAN TRAVEL
   COMMISSION

630 Fifth Ave. #611
NY, NY 10111
Phone: (212) 307-1200

VALEM CAMPING CARE
12R 16 ave de la République
Bagnolet, Paris, France 93170
Phone: 1-364-4860

EUROPE FREE
Shore/Campbell Publications
1437R Lucille Ave.
Los Angeles, CA 90026

TRAVEL EUROPE
WITH YOUR MOTORHOME
Bristol Publishing
P.O. Box 81R, Bristol, IN 46507

CARAVAN ABROAD
56R Middle St.
Brockam, Surrey,
RH3 7HW England

BRITANNIA RV RENTALS INC.
Europe, UK, Australia
Box 1333R
Jonesboro, GA 30237
Phone: 800-872-1140

INTERNATIONAL CAMPER
   EXCHANGE
P.O. Box 947R
North Bend, WA 98045

EXECUTIVE MOTORHOME
RENTALS & TOURS
Opelstrasse 28B
D-6082R Moerfelsen,
West Germany
Phone: (0 61 05) 30 37

BEST EUROPEAN TRAVEL TIPS
Meadow Brook Press,
18318R Minnetoka Blvd.
Deephaven, MN 55391

ADMIRAL CRUISES, INC.
P.O. Box 010882R
Miami, FL 33101

CAMPING ALASKA &
CANADA'S YUKON
Pacific Search Press
222R Dexter Ave. N.
Seattle, WA 98109

SANBORN MEXICAN CAR
INSURANCE
P.O. Box 1210R
McAllen, TX 79930
Phone: (512) 682-3401

RV CAMPING IN MEXICO
John Muir Publications
P.O. Box 613R
Santa Fe, NM 87504
Phone: 800-888-7504

MEXïCO (Insider's Guide)
Hippocrene Books Inc.
171 Madison Ave.
New York, NY 10016
Phone: (212) 685-4371

TIPS FOR TRAVELERS TO MEXICO
U.S. Government Printing Office
Washington, DC 20402

MEXICO TOURISM
P.O. Box 8013
Smithtown, NY 11787

PUERTO RICO TOURISM
P.O. Box 025268
Miami, FL 33102-5268
Phone: 800-223-6530
(212) 541-6630

WHERE TO GO IN AMERICA
Hippocrene Books, Inc.
171 Madison Ave.

New York, NY 10016
Phone: (212) 685-4371

DISCOVER AMERICA (State
Tourism Offices)
TIAA
2 Lafayette Centre
1133 21st St. NW
Washington, DC 20036

OTTAWA CITY TOURISM OFFICE
65 Elgin St.
Ottawa, Ont. Canada K2P OE7
Phone: (613) 237-5158

CANADA (Planning a Trip)
Hippocrene Books Inc.
171 Madison Ave.
New York, NY 10016
Phone: (212) 685-4371

CANADIAN CUSTOM OFFICE
P.O. Box 10 Station A
Toronto, Ont. M5W 1A3
Phone: (416) 973-8022
(416) 676-3643

GUIDE TO WESTERN CANADA
and GUIDE TO EASTERN
CANADA
The Globe Pequot Press
138R W. Main St.
Chester, CT 06412

TOURISM CANADA
4th Floor E
235 Queen St.
Ottawa, Ont. Canada K1A OH6

DIRECTORY OF THEME & AMUSE-
MENT PARKS and DIRECTORY
OF FREE TOURIST ATTRACTIONS
Pilot Books,
103R Cooper St.
Babylon, NY 11702
Phone: (516) 422-2225

ROAD MAPS ATLAS WHEELER
1310R Jarvis Ave.
Elk Grove, IL 60007

General RV Reading
SURVIVAL OF THE SNOWBIRDS
HOME IS WHERE YOU PARK IT.
THE RAINBOW CHASERS
ENCYCLOPEDIA FOR RVERS

Roving Press Publications
Rt 5 Box 310R
Livingston, TX 77351

TRAILER LIFE MAGAZINE
MOTORHOME MAGAZINE
RVING AMERICA'S BACKROADS
TL Enterprises
29901R Agoura Rd.
Agoura, CA 91301

Phone: 800-234-3450
CA: 800-382-3455

CHEVY OUTDOORS MAGAZINE
P.O. Box 2063R
Warren, MI 48090-9990

LA VIE NOMADE
A LA PORTEE DE TOUS
by Rollanda Dumais Masse.
(French version of this book)

Quebecor Publishers
4435R Grandes Prairies,
Montreal, Que. Canada H1R 3N4
Phone: (514) 327-6900
800-361-3946 in Canada

About $15 U.S. (including mailing)
on your Visa or Mastercard

Index

TRAVEL THE WORLD WITH HIPPOCRENE BOOKS!

HIPPOCRENE INSIDER'S GUIDES:
The series which takes you beyond the tourist track to give you an insider's view:

NEPAL
PRAKASH A. RAJ
0091 ISBN 0-87052-026-1 $9.95 paper

HUNGARY
NICHOLAS T. PARSONS
0921 ISBN 0-87052-976-5 $16.95 paper

MOSCOW, LENINGRAD AND KIEV (Revised)
YURI FEDOSYUK
0024 ISBN 0-87052-881-5 $11.95 paper

PARIS
ELAINE KLEIN
0012 ISBN 0-87052-876-9 $14.95 paper

POLAND (Second Revised Edition)
ALEXANDER T. JORDAN
0029 ISBN 0-87052-880-7 $9.95 paper

TAHITI (Revised)
VICKI POGGIOLI
0084 ISBN 0-87052-794-0 $9.95 paper

THE FRENCH ANTILLES (Revised)
ANDY GERALD GRAVETTE

The Caribbean islands of Guadeloupe, Martinique, St. Bartholomew, and St. Martin, and continental Guyane (French Guiana)

0085 ISBN 0-87052-105-5 $11.95 paper

By the same author:

THE NETHERLANDS ANTILLES:
A TRAVELER'S GUIDE

The Caribbean islands of Aruba, Bonaire, Curacao, St. Maarten, St. Eustatius, and Saba.

0240 ISBN 0-87052-581-6 $9.95 paper

HIPPOCRENE LANGUAGE AND TRAVEL GUIDES:
Because traveling is twice as much fun if you can meet new people as well as new places!

MEXICO
ILA WARNER

An inside look at verbal and non-verbal communication, with suggestions for sightseeing on and off the beaten track.

0503 ISBN 0-87052-622-7 $14.95 paper

HIPPOCRENE COMPANION GUIDES:
Written by American professors for North Americans who wish to enrich their travel experience with an understanding of local history and culture.

SOUTHERN INDIA
JACK ADLER

Covers the peninsular states of Tamil Nadu, Andhra Pradesh, and Karnataka, and highlights Goa, a natural gateway to the south.

0632 ISBN 0-87052-030-X $14.95 paper

AUSTRALIA
GRAEME and TAMSIN NEWMAN
0671 ISBN 0-87052-034-2 $16.95 paper

IRELAND
HENRY WEISSER
0348 ISBN 0-87052-633-2 $14.95 paper

POLAND
JILL STEPHENSON and ALFRED BLOCH
"An appealing amalgam of practical information, historical curiosities,
and romantic forays into Polish culture"—*Library Journal*
0894 ISBN 0-87052-636-7 $11.95 paper

PORTUGAL
T. J. KUBIAK
2305 ISBN 0-87052-739-8 $14.95 paper

ROMANIA
LYDLE BRINKLE
0351 ISBN 0-87052-634-0 $14.95 paper

THE SOVIET UNION
LYDLE BRINKLE
0357 ISBN 0-87052-635-9 $14.95 paper

THE CEMETERY BOOK
TOM WEIL
The ultimate guide to spirited travel describes burial grounds, cata-
combs, and similar travel haunts the world over (or under).
0106 ISBN 0-87052-916-1 $22.50 cloth

GUIDE TO EAST AFRICA:
KENYA, TANZANIA, AND THE SEYCHELLES (Revised)
NINA CASIMATI

0043 ISBN 0-87052-883-1 $14.95 paper

TRAVEL SAFETY:
SECURITY AND SAFEGUARDS AT HOME AND ABROAD
JACK ADLER and THOMAS C. TOMPKINS

0034 ISBN 0-87052-884-X $8.95 paper

And three books by GEORGE BLAGOWIDOW to keep you on your toes:

TRAVELER'S TRIVIA TEST:
1,101 QUESTIONS AND ANSWERS FOR THE SOPHSTICATED GLOBETROTTER

0087 ISBN 0-87052-915-3 $6.95 paper

TRAVELER'S I.Q. TEST:
RATE YOUR GLOBETROTTING KNOWLEDGE

0103 ISBN 0-87052-307-4 $6.95 paper

TRAVELER'S CHALLENGE:
SOPHISTICATED GLOBETROTTER'S RECORD BOOK

0398 ISBN 0-87052-248-5 $6.95 paper

TO PURCHASE HIPPOCRENE'S BOOKS contact your local bookstore, or write to Hippocrene Books, 171 Madison Avenue, New York, NY 10016. Please enclose a check or money order, adding $3 shipping (UPS) for the first book, and 50 cents for each of the others.

Write also for our full catalog of maps and foreign language dictionaries and phrasebooks.